W9-DEL-525

Lenore McComas Coberly
Jeri McCormick
Karen Updike

Writers Have No Age
Creative Writing
for Older Adults
Second Edition

Pre-publication
REVIEWS,
COMMENTARIES,
EVALUATIONS . . .

"**W**riters Have No Age is a personable, user-friendly, and inspiring journey through the elements of writing craft, and an exploration of the creative impulse that older adults in a group setting or working on their own will find beneficial and enjoyable in their quests to rediscover and write their own stories.

Coberly, McCormick, and Updike have the sort of warm, personable, anecdotal approach in this craft book that works particularly well with older adults. They assure their readers that they are also adults with shared concerns and a wealth of life experience, and they offer their own stories along with anecdotes and tips from well-known writers. Their approach appeals to their older readership in a respectful, conversational tone with strategies that teach them how they too might mine their life memories and turn them into creative work."

Jaimee Wriston Colbert
Assistant Professor
of Creative Writing,
Binghamton University,
State University of New York;
Author of *Climbing the God Tree*;
Winner of the Willa Cather
Fiction Prize

OCT -- '05

More pre-publication
REVIEWS, COMMENTARIES, EVALUATIONS . . .

"This warm, friendly companion offers insight, encouragement, and renewed excitement for the writer and the writing instructor. The authors provide a variety of exercises and suggestions. They also offer examples of their own writing and share the process of creation that spawned them.

As a writing teacher, I found Coberly's advice on teaching in nursing-home settings to be especially helpful and inspiring—and applicable to any teaching setting. At the core of all teaching must reside a fundamental respect for the writer and the writer's intention. These three writers practice what they preach in these pages. The writing is always clear, often poetic, and reliably helpful."

Marshall J. Cook, MA
Professor of Creative Writing,
Department of Liberal Studies and Arts,
University of Wisconsin–Madison;
Editor, *Creativity Connection Newsletter*

"This is a wonderful book for writers and would-be writers of any age. These skilled writers and teachers of writing take you through what they've learned: how to create your space, jump-start your work, mine your memory, and focus your free writing; how to pick your genre and engage your readers in your poem, essay, or story; how to revise and re-vision your work; how to get over procrastination and writer's block; how to market your work; and how to teach writing to other adults of many ages."

Robin Chapman, PhD
Professor Emerita,
University of Wisconsin–Madison

The Haworth Press®
New York • London • Oxford

NOTES FOR PROFESSIONAL LIBRARIANS AND LIBRARY USERS

This is an original book title published by The Haworth Press, Inc. Unless otherwise noted in specific chapters with attribution, materials in this book have not been previously published elsewhere in any format or language.

CONSERVATION AND PRESERVATION NOTES

All books published by The Haworth Press, Inc. and its imprints are printed on certified pH neutral, acid-free book grade paper. This paper meets the minimum requirements of American National Standard for Information Sciences-Permanence of Paper for Printed Material, ANSI Z39.48-1984.

Writers Have No Age
Creative Writing for Older Adults

Second Edition

THE HAWORTH PRESS
Titles of Related Interest

Story Writing in a Nursing Home: A Patchwork of Memories edited by Martha Tyler John

From Deep Within: Poetry Workshops in Nursing Homes edited by Carol F. Peck

Herspace: Women, Writing, and Solitude edited by Jo Malin and Victoria Boynton

The Way of the Woman Writer, Second Edition by Janet Lynn Roseman

The "Feeling Great!" Wellness Program for Older Adults by Jules C. Weiss

"You Bring Out the Music in Me": Music in Nursing Homes edited by Beckie Karras

Activities and the "Well" Elderly edited by Phyllis M. Foster

Creative Arts with Older People edited by Janice McMurray

Writers Have No Age
Creative Writing for Older Adults

Second Edition

Lenore McComas Coberly
Jeri McCormick
Karen Updike

The Haworth Press®
New York • London • Oxford

© 2005 by The Haworth Press, Inc. All rights reserved. No part of this work may be reproduced or utilized in any form or by any means, electronic or mechanical, including photocopying, microfilm, and recording, or by any information storage and retrieval system, without permission in writing from the publisher. Printed in the United States of America.

The Haworth Press, Inc., 10 Alice Street, Binghamton, NY 13904-1580.

"Take an Old Cherry Table," included in Chapter 1 of this book, first appeared in *The Christian Science Monitor,* October 23, 1998. Copyright Lenore McComas Coberly.

"A Girl Running," included in Chapter 6 of this book, placed second in the 2001 Davoren Hanna Poetry Competition, Dublin, Ireland. Copyright Jeri McCormick.

"Villanelle for Dropouts at 8:30 a.m.," included in Chapter 8 of this book, was first published in *Isthmus,* Madison, Wisconsin, 1980. Copyright Karen Updike.

"Serendipity," included in Chapter 15 of this book, first appeared in *Writer's Journal* 22(3). Copyright Lenore McComas Coberly.

"The Fellowship at Wysong's Clearing," included in Chapter 16 of this book, is taken from *The Handywoman Stories,* published by Ohio University Press/Swallow Books, Athens, Ohio, 2002. Copyright Lenore McComas Coberly.

Cover design by Marylouise E. Doyle.

Library of Congress Cataloging-in-Publication Data

Coberly, Lenore M.
    Writers have no age : creative writing for older adults / Lenore McComas Coberly, Jeri McCormick, Karen Updike.—2nd ed.
       p. cm.
    Includes bibliographical references and index.
    ISBN 0-7890-2468-3 (hard : alk. paper)—ISBN 0-7890-2469-1 (soft : alk. paper)
    1. English language—Rhetoric—Study and teaching. 2. Creative writing—Study and teaching. 3. Older people—Education. 4. Adult education. I. McCormick, Jeri. II. Updike, Karen. III. Title.
PE1404.C55 2004
808'.042'071'5—dc22

2004009809

CONTENTS

ABOUT THE AUTHORS

Lenore McComas Coberly, BS, MA, taught at the University of Wisconsin for several years and then began teaching writing in 1976. She has published two volumes of poetry, several articles and essays, and short stories in various journals. Her work has been read in the *Christian Science Monitor,* the *Wisconsin State Journal, Isthmus, Nimrod,* and the *Journal of Nanjing University* in China. Ms. Coberly was co-editor of *Heartland Journal* for seven years.

Jeri McCormick, BS, MA, has been a freelance writer and editor since 1974, a counselor since 1976, and is co-editor of *Heartland Journal.* Her poems have been published in *Wisconsin Academy Review, Poet Lore, Isthmus, Iowa Woman, Kentucky Poetry Review, Transactions, Rosebud, Cumberland Poetry Review, The Glacier Stopped Here, Byline, Poetry Ireland Review,* and others. She now teaches writing in the national Elderhostel program. Ms. McCormick lives in Madison, WI.

Karen Updike, BA, MAT, received her Master of Arts in Teaching from Harvard. She was a teacher for several years until finally becoming a freelance writing teacher and editor. Her published works include *Echoes from Mount and Plain, Sonja,* and *Off Riding.* Ms. Updike resides in Madison, WI.

Foreword

We have been given a gift and a guide.

I am pleased to present—in a manner of speaking—three talented writers who share their craft and offer ideas on how their experience can be useful to others. The authors of this book have, through years of valuable experience, discovered what it takes to spark the creative energy of older writers. They have been very mindful of what seemed to work and what didn't. Each has watched with all of the love and attention of a master teacher, but also with the critical eye of a sensitive writer, to discover what it takes to encourage individuals who have, through their lives, been so engaged in other work that they have missed the joy that comes from writing clearly, shaping important ideas, and enjoying the craftsmanship of it.

This book is a gift. It is given by those who have clearly enjoyed the time they have invested to bring a group together. They have discovered and honed the talents of their students. They have helped to shape and appreciated their students' ideas and feelings. This book is a gift given to those of us eager to learn how to stimulate creativity among older persons.

This book is also a guide that offers to one concerned about the craft of writing practical counsel on how to help others discover, within their own beings, creative capacity and how to tap the wells of experience of older writers. As a guide, the book leads the reader through the steps that have proven helpful to these three writer-teachers so that their objective analysis of what worked and what didn't could become a guide for others. This book is indeed a guide for gifted, committed, dedicated teachers.

The book is also a guide for a growing number of individuals who have taken the time and invested the energy to bring together people—many for the first time in their lives—to think about what writing is and what it expresses and what it stores up as treasures for tomorrow. This book will prove invaluable to teacher-writers as they face new opportunities and perplexing dilemmas.

The first time through, simply accept the gift, the insights, the joys, the anecdotes, and appreciate the fact that accomplished writer-teachers thought enough of you to share their experiences and what they have learned through the years.

The second time through, consider it a guide to your development of a course plan, a syllabus, an outline. As a guide, this book will take you through the geography of a good writing workshop, a classroom, a library. It will prove useful to you as you develop a course, a strategy, a style by which your skills, talents, and dedication can be brought effectively together for and with your students of all ages.

Keep it handy. You will find, as I have, numerous occasions when the authors' ideas will be immediately applicable and useful. Add it to your pens and paper, to your outlines and notes, to your diary and manuscripts. Keep it near your desk; take it to class with you.

Enjoy it as a gift; appreciate it as a guide; use it as a tool.

James T. Sykes
Former Chair
National Council on the Aging
Editor, Global Ageing

Preface

We who are older adults are potential writers, possessed of rich lodes of experience to mine. Like most people, we enjoy the experience of wrestling with things—a block of wood, a piecrust— and making beauty and order emerge from our vigorous effort. Why not wrestle with ourselves, as we have confronted and continue to confront our own lives? Writing allows us to continue to enjoy some control over our lives, to retain the sense of being the acting agent instead of the one acted upon. While some may prefer a solitary, contemplative writing method, others may choose a writing group as a place to be heard and enjoyed regularly—a place that showcases a long and rich lifetime as a proper subject for writing.

Although we survive by what we were, we stop being really alive if we rest on our laurels and do not use the skills and experiences of the past to contend with our present. The *alive* person is always in a process of growing and evolving. In a poem titled "An 80 Years Self Portrait," Alex Stevens writes, "I am content to be what I am not content to stay; / the husks untidier each spring . . ."

Writing is important to people of all ages because it is a way of exploring our inner selves—our growing, changing, evolving selves. Members of a writing workshop felt writing had aided their general sense of well-being because it had "brought them back to themselves." In his poem "Essay on Sanity," Stephen Dunn writes, "Nevertheless it is with our poems / that we must visit ourselves." Writing does bring us news about ourselves, who we really are, what we can hope to be, just as surely as newspapers bring us news of the outer world.

Saying that writing brings us back to ourselves suggests that we may have somehow lost ourselves along the way. We may have forgotten to listen to ourselves because we were so involved in taking care of others. We may not have had the courage to listen to ourselves. We may not have dared to let go of one way of being to face the uncharted land of a new way of being. Kierkegaard tells us that the greatest danger, that of losing one's own self, may pass off as if it were nothing, while every other loss is sure to be noticed. Coming to know oneself and others more deeply through writing is the very reason for the humanities in general and literature in particular. Without the lubricating or leavening influence of art flowing through our lives, helping us to change ourselves, we do stop growing, we do lose ourselves.

But if when we explore our past we insist on literally transcribing things as we think they really were, we will miss the excitement of transforming experience into art. At first we do find common ground in similar memories. Many of us have walked the country road to school, smelled inkwells and sweeping compound, or watched trolleys clank along their tracks. We first write of safe things with which we all can easily identify. Gradually, however, we come to value not our similarities but our differences, each unique viewpoint, descriptive eye, narrative gift. Wonder of wonders, we find we are not all of a piece.

Paying attention to the past, reinspecting it, or looking at it again, teaches us to look at the present with sharper, more accurate, observation. Reinspecting the person we were in the past, when we flourished with the zest, spontaneity, and autonomy characteristic of untrammeled childhood, reminds us of that way of being again. Re-creating the past self in stories, we find we remember a wealth of sensory details and images that enliven writing and deepen our understanding. The arts, including writing, order, inspire, and enable us. They order the confusing, chaotic images and events of our amorphous, unstructured past and help us perceive meaning in what is random, unpredictable, and impersonal.

We should not be surprised that the process of writing is so energizing, so life enhancing. Maxine Kumin (1979) writes in *To Make a Prairie,* "You begin with the chaos of events and impressions and feelings, you marshal your arguments and metaphors, pound and hammer them into shape and form, feel the marvelous informing order emerge from it and feel reborn!"

Good writing for all of us is close to the wellspring. It comes up to us, if we let it, through the pipes of the unconscious. It percolates through the ground of our being, refreshing us, rinsing away the arid encrustations of mask and role, our outer rooms, and re-stores us to ourselves. In this book we have put together some of our own best writing and teaching ideas and methods to help you enjoy the re-creation and stimulation of writing, whatever your age.

Karen Updike

Chapter 1

Why We Write

Jeri McCormick

Those of us who come to writing have always cared about words. As children we felt their power in nursery rhymes and stories. We took delight in the Burma Shave signs along the road, one of which I've remembered for more than fifty years: "Don't stick your elbow / out too far / or it may go home / in another car." We writers took in language and savored it long before we started to shape it ourselves. Having been readers and listeners from childhood on, we eventually come to see how words can further serve us, take us deeper into our own hearts and minds, give focus and order to our lives, and then pass on our thoughts to others through our creations.

This decision to take up the pen comes slowly for many. Other callings and commitments bring postponement of that rendezvous with the writer's desk. As teachers of writing, we have encountered numerous would-be writers who managed to hold onto their dream for decades before they could actually "clear the decks" enough to act on it. Tillie Olsen, the fiction writer, has written about this struggle in her book *Silences* (2003). Fortunately, the dreamers we have met in our classes did not simply give up and plop down in front of the television screen for their final decades. They kept that writing goal and pursued it upon retirement, some in their eighties and nineties by the time the opportunity for sufficient leisure and solitude came. We have found that age does not matter, only the will to write.

What accounts for this die-hard determination? Plenty of other ways to keep busy in this life are available. Why do some persist with the writer's dream in the face of so many obstacles? The rewards are profound. Anyone who writes letters or enters musings in a journal knows how beneficial that bit of thought gathering can be. Writing brings news of ourselves; and, if we're doing it for the added purpose of showing someone else, it shares that news mind to mind, person to person. The more we know about ourselves and one another, the more empowered we feel, the better able to understand the human condition. It has been said that we write for the love of man and in praise of God. The search for meaning is common to everyone, writer or not; but for writers, understanding is especially rich and satisfying when that search is carried on through language.

We know that people are often drawn to writing with no precise aim in mind. They sense that they'll somehow feel better if they write. Why is this so? This need to write often intensifies in the mature years when looking back and assessing the choices made over a lifetime. Clarification of *who, when, how, why,* and *where* comes through putting memories into words. We find out who our past selves were. A review of events, their causes and outcomes, helps us understand our place in the world, thus helping define our worth and our legacy. With time and experience intervening, the writer is better equipped to bring perspective and meaning to those earlier events, infusing them, perhaps, with maturity and even wisdom.

Writing can save us from boring others with our favorite stories. We've all met storytellers who never tire of repeating themselves. It takes great patience to sit through such repetitions, even when the story is basically interesting and we enjoyed it the first time. Writing provides another mode for retelling those good stories. Reliving comes with retelling, and the crafting with words on a page allows us to savor the experience once again. Others will better appreciate that story when they can choose to read it rather than sit captive to it in a monologue. Writing helps refine the story and makes us better storytellers; we acquire selectivity, the ability to choose what to tell and what not to tell.

Like everyone else, writers must function in the here and now. Language performs a concrete service as an organizing tool for living day to day. After all, we can't focus entirely on what we've already experienced in the past, however valuable that review may be; we must also deal with the ongoing flow of change. To quote an astute participant in a writing Elderhostel, "Change, like mange, creeps upon you." Life does not stall and go into neutral at a certain age. It keeps on going in one way or another, in the environment, in technology and medicine, in the growth cycles of children and grandchildren, in institutions and laws, and in nation-states. We need to read, listen, and observe a great deal to keep up with the world; and for some of us it helps to record in writing our frustrations and satisfactions along the way. Recording thoughts on the page gives us a way to lighten our mental burdens, a way to "talk back." In this age of high stress, everyone has to find some means of relief. Physical exercise helps, and we certainly need it, but we also need the mental sort that weighs and measures events and ideas. For this mind work, some will be content with verbal exchanges, talking things over with friends; but for those drawn to writing, deeper understanding comes from putting thoughts down on paper. These recordings, whatever the chosen form—essay, poem, fiction, or unshaped paragraphs—keep us in touch with ourselves, give us a grounding we cannot afford to lose, a unity that keeps us whole.

Anyone who has lived a long time knows that other people have contributed to his or her longevity. Who among us could get along totally alone in the world? We've all had to depend on others, and recognizing this, we take pleasure in acknowledging the key people in our lives through writing. The same is true of places and events, personal and historical. For a writer, all of these lived-through accumulations seem to require telling about. It's true that we often do just that in conversations, but writing about them gives a more lasting way to share the highlights of our lives. Stories put down on paper will likely reach a wider audience, be passed along to a later generation, or if published, be placed in the hands of readers whom the writer has never met. So we write to share, and in doing so we gain a place in human history—a quiet, obscure place, perhaps, lived far from celebrities and power wielders, but nevertheless a vivid, meaningful place where hearts and minds connect.

Not all writers set out to plumb humanity's profound truths through their efforts. Some just want to tell a good story or outline the key events in the family saga or take delight in amusing word games, such as limericks. All of these are worthy reasons to write. They illustrate how writing can be fun, rather than a nose-to-the-grindstone struggle. In all cases, light or serious, there comes the satisfaction of getting words down. And for anyone who stays with the practice, a broader interest may arise with more varied pursuits unanticipated at the outset. The results might be for the writer's own eyes at first, but the possibility exists that eventually those words may be refined for others to see as well.

What more can writing do? It can stimulate and enliven, adding spark to our minds and our lives. It promotes creativity, that high form of human activity. To spend time with a writer is to see that layers exist beyond what meets the eye. Here is a person with a mind gainfully employed, we surmise, one who never has to contend with boredom. Imagination is on tap; time is in short supply. Thus the process itself is reason enough to take up writing. It brings adventure. Writers at work travel far beyond a room and a desk; we take off across time and space, relive former lives, try out others' lives, make up new ones. There is no end to where explorers with words will go or what we will find.

Chapter 2

Alone or in a Group:
Do Writers Need One Another?

Lenore McComas Coberly

I was a young aspiring writer busy with the needs of a large family when I joined The Wisconsin Fellowship of Poets. We met twice yearly at different locations around the state to hear one another and to talk about poetry.

At one of my first meetings in Shawano I happened to sit with Mae Baber at lunch. She was tall, slim, regal, with the wind-toughened skin of the farmer's wife. She smiled at me and commented on the poem which I had read that morning. I exclaimed with admiration for her memory, knowing that my poem was not great. She explained to me that she used the twice-a-year meetings to refuel her muse for the long solitudes of a northern farm.

In the years I was privileged to know her, I came to admire her complex poetry about everyday events and scenes. I also came to know that my own muse needed refueling by being in the presence of people like me, people who must write to be truly alive.

Seeking a place in an organized group or organizing a small group of your own is a way to find fellowship that makes the writing life whole. Libraries can help you find a group, notices of bookstore readings are invitations to be among writers, and learning about local writers and talking with them is a direct route to groups. But there are potential pitfalls.

Well-meaning friends may want to meet with you and hear your writing. They are happy to have a writing friend even though they are not writers. This is fine, but don't take their comments and suggestions seriously. You must keep your own counsel. Meeting with other writers will help you be yourself as a writer.

Then there are "writers" who, in fact, want to have written but are not motivated to write. A group can encourage and nurture one or two of these types, but they can be a drain. One way to keep the group going, especially the dreamers, is to make assignments at each meeting. However, it is important that these be optional. Some members of the group will be deeply into a writing project and should not digress.

Group members who mistake talk for writing are difficult to incorporate. They may take up time talking about what they are going to write or what they have written, which is usually slight. They need to be told firmly that the group is there to hear what has been written, not what might be written or excuses for what has not been written.

Occasionally the tendency to take time with explanations arises from a genuine lack of confidence. The group can help these writers by interrupting them with eager expectation for hearing what they have written. In one group, a frustrated listener exclaimed, "Read the damn story!" which brought forth laughter but got the writer to start reading. That exclamation served the group well for many years.

When it is not possible for writers to physically get together, a round-robin is a rich substitute. I know a group of writers who met at a writing Elderhostel at the Green Lake Conference Center in Wisconsin who have had a round-robin for more than ten years. They come from all over the country to this Elderhostel whenever they can, but at times some cannot be present. So they mail manuscripts to one another, passing each one along to every member of the group.

The most successful round-robins I have known are organized by one person and start out with invitations to five to ten writers to join. The leader puts his or her manuscript in a manila envelope and encloses a list of participants with addresses and includes a brief letter with writers' news. After the manuscript has gone around twice, it is removed by the author. These carefully read and critiqued works are real teaching tools for the solitary writer.

Electronic means of "getting together," in the absence of a live group, provide encouragement to writers. Richard Roe, a leader at a Writers' Elderhostel and other writers' workshops, has enjoyed many ways of communicating with other writers when he is not at work as historian and analyst at the Wisconsin Legislative Reference Bureau. Richard states:

> With the widespread use of personal computers, many writers have found that e-mail is a good way to send works in progress to each other. We can exchange material with favored individuals and form an e-mail group similar to manuscript groups that meet face to face and round-robins that use regular mail. I belong to Entendres, an online gathering of poets who send their work via e-mail for comments and criticism.
>
> Each writer sends a poem to all twelve poets on an address list simultaneously, and each response also goes to the entire list. The majority of members usually answer within seventy-two hours. I recommend one poem at a time to other groups to keep from getting bogged down in material to critique.
>
> Because e-mail systems and providers vary, strange things can happen to poems in cyberspace. Your line breaks are not their line breaks. Word-processing programs are not necessarily built for poetry. Sometimes a poem does not reach all of the members because a system is down, there's a virus, or a "mailbox" is too full. Sometimes, one of us hits the delete key at the wrong time and the poem and comments disappear. However, one can always ask the author for another copy.
>
> In spite of human and electronic glitches, poetry by e-mail proves to be an effective way to get comments on one's work. For some members, the critiques have worked well. Their poems have won prizes in contests or were published.
>
> As in round-robins and manuscript groups, there's no room for personal enmity in e-mail groups. We expect civil behavior. We are cautious in accepting new members. Right now we have twelve, and that's quite enough. As it is, some members are very active, while others participate very little. Getting poems out, reading them, and commenting on them depends on our individual schedules.

E-mail does not and cannot replace live manuscript groups. The give and take of conversation and discussion is irreplaceable. Yet, Entendre members have provided information on publications, contests, and "zines" (online magazines). We have discussed ethical issues in writing and publishing and experiences that may not have much to do with writing.

Retirement communities are ideal for writers' groups, as are neighborhoods. Following is an essay I wrote about the need for a group and a poem about a long-standing group. Even your group will be grist for your writer's mill!

We Leave Behind Our Other Lives
An Essay

Lenore McComas Coberly

We were driving home from the budget theater after seeing *Ocean's 11* when my granddaughters and I began to discuss why people enjoy seeing violence, crime, and a woman with poor taste in men on the screen. None of us doubted the positive response of the audience.

The most straightforward view came from the youngest, who had just had her own play produced at the middle school. "They like to see Brad Pitt," she announced. Remembering Leslie Howard in *Gone with the Wind,* I knew she was onto something.

Our high school senior pronounced the movie sick, decadent, and chauvinistic, which I could not refute. A midgeneration view held it to be the Robin Hood story. We secretly feel, she said, that the rich *should* be robbed for the good of the poor.

I, who had mistaken *Ocean's 11* for a sequel with Roman numerals, had, nonetheless, been struck by the ending of the film in which eleven men line up after the successful heist, looking at a Las Vegas casino from across a court. Suddenly illuminated fountains erupt and the camera shifts to show their faces—old, young, handsome, plain, black, white, Asian, suave, even naive—just before the group begins to disperse, one by one, to return to everyday life, secure both in friendship and in wealth.

But the wealth is not visible. That, for me, summed up the intention of the writer and filmmakers. They had formed a group that shared excitement and accomplishment, however deviant. That was what we were being told by the filmmaker.

Viewers like to see groups of people who are loyal to one another and to the group. Even the merry men of Sherwood Forest captivate us this way. War movies such as *Black Hawk Down* and *We Were Soldiers* show, above all, comradeship. The success of the *Seinfeld* and *Friends* series on television may have been due to the charm of the community more than the wit, which was considerable.

If we like to see this level of friendship in movies, we like even more to experience it, whoever we are. Writers are not exceptions. Fifteen years ago I invited ten writers to bring a brown bag lunch and manuscripts in progress to my house at 12:30 every other Wednesday. I made coffee and waited. They came, young and old, men, women, fiction writers, poets, and essayists, some taking time off from work. They stayed until dinnertime. Fifteen years later, we are skilled writers who enjoy one another's successes at snatching writing riches from the jaws of rejection. In short, I guess that makes us human, even those who are as handsome as Brad Pitt.

On my seventy-fifth birthday the members of the group wrote a collection of remembrances. One exulted that "here we leave our other lives behind." Indeed we do, and find ourselves free to be writers.

Take an Old Cherry Table

on a Wednesday afternoon,
crowd the chairs around,
gather a family of friends,
and let the talk begin.
Add some apricots, peanuts, coffee,
mix with premeditated metaphor
and wit to fit the day,
until everything starts to rise,

filling crevasses of lonely rejection
that will never be so deep again,
and the table glows.

Lenore McComas Coberly

A woman in New Jersey wrote to me, "Our writing group reads your poem before each meeting!" And there is something here, in this writers' gangland, that has no need for Las Vegas. An old cherry table will do.

Robin Chapman, a widely published poet and Emeritus Professor of Communicative Disorders at the University of Wisconsin–Madison, has long participated in manuscript critique groups and acted as a leader at writers' conferences. She has found the groups indispensable in her writing life. I asked her to describe her experience.

Kindred Spirits and Acute Listeners
Robin Chapman

A writers' group teaches you the unique quality of every voice, the irreplaceableness of each speaker at the table, the fascination of an individual's motion of mind and music of speech. And if your writing group includes people of varied voice, place, and age, the worlds and words brought to the table stretch your life to places you've never seen—a seminary, an occult bookstore, a dairy farm, a West Virginia creek, a physicists' town. To structures you may not have encountered, of litany, rap, chants, and spells. To others' life-and-death facts of harsh winters, spring floods, mercury spills. To the things never told to anyone else. You hear stories and poems and plays and novels of town intrigue, family combat, and lifelong yearnings that leave you laughing and crying and gasping, your understanding of the human condition deepened, your spirit enlivened, your courage to write renewed.

I've been a member of many versions of writers' groups and learned much from each. But most important, most enduring, has been the decade-long writing group I've belonged to that meets every other Wednesday. We gather around the cherry-wood table; or, in summers, around the round patio table on the screened-in porch, to spend the afternoon. Our hostess has set up the coffee and tea in the kitchen. On the table are new magazines and journals, announcements of writing contests, postcards and letters from group members who've moved, still present in spirit at the table. We bring our lunches, and our poems, stories, novels, plays. Outside, the crows and rabbits gather.

Talk and crumbs fly; we eat; we laugh; we tell what's happening in our lives; we get up to get more coffee; and then a person is called on, and the work begins. We read what we have written and listen hard to one another. A's prodigal puns and sly humor, B's verb-packed adjectives doubling the action in the narrative, C's story of power struggles in the medical world, her doctor-nurse dialogue crackling. D's essays delighting us at every eye-popping, gut-busting, death-defying turn. E's meditations on spring riding, her laugh-out-loud family struggles. F's love of nature, song, and the tango braiding in his preacher's-son voice. G's love of painting and the Southwest coloring new myths. H's edgy narrators—bureaucrats, country singers, speakers to the moon. I's litanies, elegies, leaps, love poems. J's memories of childhood, reading Superman comics and *Lad: A Dog* under the covers. K's Appalachian stories, the point of view shifting from woman to man to child as complexity layers and the plots twist. Her apple cake or corn bread recipes make our mouths water and allow us to bake them later.

We have brought what we wrote in haste between work and dinner, or in terror of setting it down on the page, or in desperation at having nothing else to bring, or in spurts of coffeehouse note making, or in steady mornings of reflection in a writing room. We have printed out copies for everyone on our laser printers, or typed two copies on the backs of old novel drafts to share. Some of us have rearranged our workdays to be here, rearranged our jobs to have more mornings open to the writing life, given up writing time to bring our work to this table, these listeners.

We say what we've heard—where the story or poem pulled us in, made something happen; delighted or surprised or moved us. We say how we interpret the metaphors, understand the relationships of the characters, the moment of the poem, the possibility for action in the play. We debate character, dialogue, and setting. Ask to be shown, not told. Ask for more, or for less. Wonder about order of events, about line breaks, section breaks, and commas. Ask if second person—or first plural, or third— might be better. Ask if it's really necessary to say something, rather than leave it to the reader to discover. Ask if the first section is scaffolding and should go, if the last section should be first.

We are at work, giving steady and thoughtful attention to the words we hear, the worlds they construct. Some advice we take; some we set aside. We are solitary writers, gathered together in communal respect for words and one another's keen editorial eyes; sharing the joy of being heard, the despairs and triumphs of shaping the work, getting it out into the world.

Chapter 3

The Work Begins

Jeri McCormick

You've already begun. You've been reading about writing and noting the styles of writers you admire; now you're about to launch a process that takes you directly into the writer's work. You're starting a mental process of visiting with yourself. Writing will take you deep into your own mind, tapping memory and imagination as you go. Your powers of observation will be stretched, your senses put to work, and your capacity for empathy heightened. You will explore what you know and what you believe, after all these years of living in the world. You'll relive where you've been and make some sense of where you are now. This powerful assessment of who you are in the world will be enhanced by the amazing tool that does so much for us: language— your language.

As with any other skill or art form, you must start at the beginning and work your way into a practice that promotes improvement; then, if all goes well, you might enjoy mastery. No guarantees can be found, but we can name plenty of examples of people for whom hard work has paid off. What about talent? Everyone wonders about that, and you're perhaps thinking that you don't have it; or, conversely, you may believe that you have plenty of it, soon to be revealed. It's most helpful if you simply shelve the notion of talent, let it remain among the mysteries we can't explain, and go ahead with some concrete activity that is useful for writers. John Gardner, the novelist, said it's hard work that counts, something any dedicated, persevering person can do. Gustave Flaubert saw talent as a kind of patience and originality as an effort of will and of intense observation.

Older people have learned many things along the way, some of which we may have to unlearn when we become serious about a new activity. In starting to write, we must scrap the idea that an author sits down to the task and proceeds sentence by sentence, page by page, beginning to end, and then the work is done. For nearly every writer, that first product is only the beginning, as you will discover in the pages ahead.

First, you will need to assemble certain items. A writer needs tools. Pen and paper will do, or whatever automated equipment appeals to you: word processor, typewriter, computer; plus a good dictionary and thesaurus for checking words and their uses. You may also need a designated place to work, bearing in mind that many possibilities exist. Whether it's a majestic rolltop desk, the kitchen table, a past-its-prime card table, or a beanbag lap pad, your writing surface should feel right to you. It should provide you with a retreat, a kind of inner sanctum that allows full concentration. Set up good lighting for that space and you're ready to begin. This station will bring you many happy returns as you practice your craft; use it often, every day if possible.

At the same time, allow yourself the flexibility to write in other places as the situation demands: at the dentist's waiting room, on the bus, seated on a park bench. Carry a small notebook or a set of note cards to pull from your pocket or purse. Using these, you can capture the immediacy of an idea or observation, and write down its essence for fleshing out later when you're back at your home base. Perhaps you've heard stories of writers resorting to paper napkins, the backs of checks, grocery receipts, any odds and ends of paper at hand; it has happened to us and may well happen to you.

Plan a work schedule to go with your tools and space. You may not be able to adhere doggedly to a daily timetable, but choose a period that works for you most days. It will help support a structure that keeps you writing. Such a structure is important for the continuing writer as well as the beginner. We must not allow the many demands on our lives to use up our days entirely. Neglecting writing day after day takes us out of our much-needed practice time, distancing us from our good intentions, so that eventually we lose the drive that got us going in the first place. This loss of momentum will sound familiar to anyone who has vowed to learn something new—piano playing, perhaps, or tennis—and then failed to follow through with the necessary practice. Progress requires effort and determination, as you know by now, and having a schedule sets a framework that helps ensure that progress. Many writers give only one or two hours a day to their craft, yet they have turned out multiple books. Some do this early in the morning, before beginning the day's employment or launching into family duties. William Stafford, an acclaimed American poet, worked at 5:00 a.m. before his family rose and his academic day began. Flexibility is essential, however, even when a schedule is in place, and you may occasionally find yourself working at midnight when your preferred time is 8:00 a.m.

Say you've arranged a work space, assembled the tools, and set up a daily schedule for writing. Now what? The time has come to move beyond the preparation stage and get down to work. If you have an idea that's already pressing to be written, proceed with it. It might be a memory, an opinion, or an observation—something that keeps coming to mind. The authors of this book have all had occasion to jot down ideas based on observations while pursuing other activities. Lenore wrote "Miss Carrollene Tells a Story" after seeing an auto repair sign ("Ramage Auto Repair") out in the country; Jeri wrote about a ladybug making its way across a rock beach; Karen wrote about horseback riding, using phrases that came to her out in the fields. We have learned to get it down on paper, writing quickly and freely, on the scene, if possible. Using those spontaneous notes, we later developed the finished work.

While creating your own first draft, you need not worry about grammar, punctuation, or organization. Double spacing and using only one side of the paper will make it easier to read later and to edit on the page. Keep in mind that this is the *vision* stage of writing; *revision* will come later when you return to the draft with an editor's eye. Likewise, format decisions will come later, when you decide whether your draft should evolve into a story, a poem, or an essay. In the appendix to this book you will find a checklist to help you with editing your work. Chapter 7 will aid in choosing the format that seems right for it.

Bad writing is bound to happen, and it may happen frequently, even to those who have enjoyed considerable success. Learn to forgive yourself when you write badly. Remember that it takes a lot of rotten work to move on to something better. This acceptance of falling short of what you had hoped to achieve leads to the flip side of expectations, where you must be careful about becoming too satisfied with your results. Watch out for the quick and easy success at the outset; it may be a misleading fluke. Enjoy it if it happens, but understand that you still have hard work ahead of you.

At times, starting off with "bad" writing is simply part of the process that gets you going. One fine short story writer begins a new story with what she calls the "Dick and Jane" method, in which she gives the curt essentials in a simple, child-like style and later returns to the draft to embellish it with the details that flesh out the story.

What if you don't have an idea, but you want to begin your writing practice? Try this. Bring a bottle of vanilla to your desk and take a whiff. (Any odor-producing substance will work for this exercise—shoe polish, mouthwash, cinnamon, mint, soap, coffee, menthol, a pine branch, a new leather wallet.) Give yourself eight minutes (you might use a kitchen timer) to write anything that comes to mind after taking in that fragrance. A sensory stimulus is particularly useful for getting you started; the sense of smell is evocative since it is one of the earliest ways people experience their environment. As infants we smell numerous things and those odors incite feelings of various kinds. We continue to use this olfactory sense to take in our surroundings and express our reactions over a lifetime. As writers, we need to call on all the senses to bring our message to the reader; they give us a human way of sharing.

The only rule for this sensory assignment, and indeed any other assignment, is that you must write *something,* aiming to fill those eight minutes. You may even write, "I can't think of anything to write," but you must keep your pen moving until the bell rings. Remember that it doesn't have to be perfect and it need not be "a big idea." Ideas should emerge from your life; abstractions can be ineffectual if not grounded and made real to the reader. It's fine to write a list, some phrases, a paragraph, a joke, a reminiscence, anything that comes to mind. Allow yourself to veer off track and see where your writing takes you. Discovery is your goal. This is how you find out what is really on your mind. You may choose to use only a small portion of your freewriting draft for further development, but you will have found the meat of your message.

When you stop, don't assess the results right away. Put the draft away and return to it in a few days. For now, simply enjoy the success of having written. Do it again tomorrow and the next day, as often as you need a jump start with words. The other senses—sight, sound, touch, and taste—offer plenty of additional options for getting you going. Make lists for each of them and choose from one of the lists when you need something to write about. For example, your sound list might include church bell, telephone, passing truck, baby crying, glass breaking, and dog barking. In the appendix to this book you will find other exercises, offering ways to get you started or keep you going with your daily practice.

As you work, try to see writing as a kind of calling that stays with you all times of day and night, not just when you're sitting at your desk. Your interest in becoming a writer at this stage of your life probably reflects your unconscious understanding of this full-time mind-set. You've been a writer all along, observing the world and trying to understand yourself as an agent in it; it's just that you haven't yet written down what you've learned. Now your time has come. Let this new commitment prompt you to observe even more closely and bring all the self-understanding you can muster to the task of word crafting.

Chapter 4

Writing's a Snap

Karen Updike

There's really no need to create a separate space for writing. Some folks surround themselves with powerful personal talismans, sufficient supplies, and even protected time. But any hour or two you can squeeze in, preferably as close to the deadline as you can cut it, is sufficient to produce a piece torn from your inner soul, wooed from the distant parts of your true self. Never discount the profound advantage of anxiety, the salutary aspect of your old friend the adrenaline rush, designated, I believe, by some eighteenth-century wag, as the panic button.

If you have trouble resisting the seductive call of a cleared desk, get out that pile of bills you've been meaning to pay and perform your customary triage into three distinct categories against the day when you will actually write those checks, lick those stamps. Even though it always smells faintly of that relative you didn't care for, you could work at the guest room writing table. Just clear it of those photographs you've been meaning to frame and get going. For good luck, select your most favorite writing object to take with you, say your special thinking stone, a cool white sphere from the North Sea, to press between your smooth palm and your fevered brow as your thoughts start to flow.

Preliminary reading is an excellent, really top-notch way to warm to your work. After all, that is what the words you write will in time become, material piled at someone else's bedside table. Get out that pile of unread *New Yorkers*. You might as well turn to the best this decade of our tired old world has to offer. Scan those tables of contents for your favorite authors and read their stories, not merely as a reader but more specifically as a reader who writes. Read them a second, even a third time, to note the use of verbs, images, and the classic unities of time and place. Skim if you will, clip if you must, several choice cartoons a friend might enjoy at lunch.

Speaking of lunch, nothing could be more writerly. Think of those luminaries who frequented the Parisian cafés along the Boule des Ecrives in the early twentieth century. Think of the masterpieces they produced: *Remembrance of Things Past* and *Singin' in the Rain*. Don't think of the ones they might have written had they not been so attached to their cups of espresso.

If you have cats who want in or dogs begging to go out, get that taken care of before you actually start to write. Being interrupted in medias res can be deadly. Might as well get that dog walk in while the sun is high and at its warmest at noon in winter so the exhausted little beasts will snore themselves into oblivion while you create. Besides, it is good to stretch your limbs after sitting still reading for so long—brings the blood to the head again where it belongs.

Inside again, a pot of tea and some buttered toast will do nicely for a little pick-me-up, preferably something caffeinated so you don't go drowsy with contentment after all that fresh air and exercise. Sit in the chair with the best view to plan your piece—a wingback serves well for propping a lolling head and looking contemplative. No paper and pencil are necessary at this point anyway. You can always retrieve those stumbled-upon insights when you retreat to that stuffy guest room and actually commit words to paper.

Now is your time to dream your piece into existence, just as when a child, after sandlot baseball and hours of pumping bikes or swings into heady torrents of speed and rushing wind, you fell into bed too tired to actually complete the Lord's Prayer, or any prayer for that matter. You merely convulsed momentarily with your large *intention* of praying, and drifted off before anyone's will was done, on earth or in heaven.

If you find yourself dozing off now, as an adult, listen to your body. It's telling you something. No one can be expected to write unrefreshed. You've plenty of time. Prop yourself up in bed and make a few notes about how you could start and what you will say when you wake up with a clear head. Don't be alarmed if you find yourself doodling acanthus leaves around the edges of your paper. Just keep that pencil moving. Eventually it will mean something.

Chapter 5

Come to Your Senses

Karen Updike

How many of us as children were admonished: Come to your senses! Straighten up! Be alert! Think things through! Do right, for goodness sake, always for the sake of goodness. Not bad advice today, for writers, but for an altogether different reason. Coming to your senses, using your senses, will enrich, not homogenize, your experiences and your writing. It certainly will make your work good and vivid, maybe even publishable.

I watched an early morning paperboy on his route and marveled at how attuned he was to every sound, even to my steps on the other side of the street behind him. I thought that in a primitive world, a person of such keen hearing could surely anticipate predators and live to propagate other sharp listeners like himself. His sensory awareness functioned to protect him; a writer uses it to write well.

Teachers often ask students to project themselves into the life of a Helen Keller or a George Shearing to experience vicariously deafness or blindness and thereby appreciate the richness and value of their own complete sensory apparatus. Often the point is made that if one sense is lost, others grow more acute. But there is also sensory deficit of another kind. After seeing the confusion and distress of an autistic child in a busy crowded classroom, I thought how instructive it would be to teach the importance of sensory awareness by asking students to identify with the confusion experienced by those who suffer from sensory overload and cannot sort out surrounding stimuli. Even for those not so afflicted, in the complexity of the modern world it is often necessary to turn off, or down, music, programs or cell phones to find the peace to listen to ourselves and create. Artur Rubenstein's wife is said to have listened to him play the piano from out in the hall so she would be able to listen without being under the magic spell his presence held for her.

Another way to realize the importance of using all your senses when you write is assign yourself the task of looking out any open window in your home and describing all you observe, hear, smell, taste, or touch. Try focusing on one sense per writing session. One student took this suggestion so seriously that she dutifully ticked off an image suggested by each sense at four different stopping points on a walk around her farm's pasture. Needless to say the piece took on a slightly formulaic quality.

What writers want to do in making a poem or telling a story is to open themselves up to all their senses, but remain able to select, assemble, and control those images to convey their meaning. In *The Long Quiet Highway* (1994), Natalie Goldberg advises using a technique of focusing on sensory input from the here and now, which she perfected in learning Buddhist meditation, but which we can all practice to good effect by writing more and writing often. Writers sort out and make images of as many sensory experiences as are available to them, and they do so in as specific, concrete, and particular words as possible, without overstepping the boundaries of clarity and conciseness. They will open the window wide to throw out most general, abstract or summary words, concepts, or statements.

In their anthology *Understanding Poetry* (1976), Cleanth Brooks and Robert Penn Warren suggest that presenting a subject concretely is the fundamental method of literature. They define the root meaning of abstract literally as an idea "drawn away from" the thing being considered, whereas the root meaning of concrete means "grown together," sensory images grown together or clustered together in a poem or story to *imply* meaning rather than *state* it directly:

> For instance, a novel or a play tells a particular story of particular people and does not merely give general comments on human nature. It presents individual human beings and pres-

ents them in action. Poetry, even more than other literary forms, makes use of *particular* images and incidents for presenting its ideas.

Imagery is the representation in poetry of any sense experience. I remember trying to digest that, when as a student teacher I had to prepare a lesson on haiku for eighth graders. At that time I was only defining images as something visual, and I was further encumbered by the misconception that all poetic images were supposed to be beautiful, refined, and uplifting. When confronted with Basho's frog plopping into an old pond, and the subsequent water sound, I didn't know what to make of it. First of all it was not visual like a snapshot, and second it was not pretty. Whatever was the poet trying to say by telling me that a frog jumped into an old pond? Gradually I came to understand that the images in a haiku, usually seasonal but not always visual, are often also about sound or taste or texture or fragrance, and that they always imply something abstract, which always remains unspoken, about the brevity of life, the complexity of longing, or the identification with and appreciation for the exquisite natural world.

The story of how the taste of one small crumb of madeleine prompted for Marcel Proust his long novel *Remembrance of Things Past* is well-known. The sense of smell is said to guide fish back to their spawning grounds and butterflies on their migrations. Select several spices from your cupboard and use them to generate a list of possible stories prompted by an odor. So might the senses guide you down the halls of memory to make stories from the major and minor dramas enacted there.

Chapter 6

Mining Your Memory

Jeri McCormick

HISTORY IS NOT FINISHED WITH US

The past is still with us. We've all emerged from events that go back thousands of years, bringing to each of us a long, long story. Those stories, though deeply rooted in time, are sometimes accessible when we look for them. Curiosity got me going on such a search for family roots. I wanted to see Ulster, the transient home of my Scotch-Irish mother's eighteenth-century ancestors; and I felt equally drawn to the west of Ireland, the turf of my husband's emigrant forebears who left for America during the Great Famine. I was fortunate enough to visit both, but my pilgrimage to the latter was especially productive.

I arrived in western Ireland soon after the 1995 launch of a Famine Museum, built on a former landlord's estate in County Roscommon 150 years after the famine. Here I saw the haunting evidence of a dreadful time and was transported through imagination to the lives of tenant cottiers who became a beleaguered and displaced populace. Continuing my research in Dublin, I read dozens of accounts, including some recorded during an oral history field project in which the descendents of survivors were interviewed early in the twentieth century. Most responses had been dictated in Irish, but many have been translated into English.

Reading these accounts of survival and loss—of death, disease, eviction, and flight from the homeland—I decided to take on this heartrending spectacle as subject matter for my own writing. I lo-

Mass evictions during the Great Famine in nineteenth-century Ireland left thousands of cottages abandoned and roofless. A million people died from starvation and disease and an additional two million fled their homeland. A team of twentieth-century field workers interviewed descendents of the survivors and put their stories into writing, stored by the Irish Folklore Commission in archives at University College–Dublin. The poem "A Girl Running" is based on an account from these manuscripts. (*Source:* Composite illustration prepared by Amy Kittleson from contemporary famine sketches.)

cated and went through lengthy bibliographies to line up information from a variety of sources and viewpoints. Then I began to write, using the stories that seemed most vivid, often the most wrenching. My interest widened as I worked, moving from a narrow family focus to the overall tragic scene across half a decade in Ireland's history.

This kind of delving brought a range of feelings, compassion, admiration, awe, and anger, which I hoped to kindle in other readers as they had been kindled in me. Poetry seemed the way to do it, mostly narrative poems telling about the people of the time, often in voices I imagined they might have used. The poem form would be succinct, I decided, yet evocative; informational, yet personal. Out of this came a poetry collection in progress that I call *Gnawbone Voices*.

Within this collection, I include the account of a baker's son who, along with his father, was accosted out on the streets because of flour-dust smells on their clothing; the musings of a woman carrying her dead daughter tied to her back as she walked to the graveyard; the advice of an overworked gravedigger who advocated hinge-bottom coffins for reuse; a curate who described his grim day among the outcast poor living in ditches. One of the poems, "A Girl Running," was the recipient of a major prize awarded by the Davoren Hanna Poetry Competition in Dublin in 2001. I include the poem here:

A Girl Running

She materializes alongside our carriage,
    a girl of twelve, we surmise, barefoot
        and garbed in a man's tattered coat.

Keeping the pace maintained by our horses,
    she focuses ahead, the coat fully buttoned,
        hands crossed to clasp wrists, cantering

unswervingly at our side. I tell her to save
    her breath, that we will give her nothing.
        Traveling here on business for the Crown,

we cannot furnish alms in this bogland of need;
    nor can we condone coins that are not contracted
        through honest work. Still, the girl runs,

never looking at us, never speaking to us,
    on and on in that garment of encumbrance,
        her thin face reddening, hair a moist tangle,

she moves with undiminished speed on naked legs
    that spin like spokes in uncanny harmony
        with our wheels. At a rise in the road

near Killaloe she acquires a rattling cough,
    sputters and hacks through the Shannon mist.
        My associate frowns, leans forward, pulls

a fourpenny from his pocket. I forgive him.
A sprint for survival means something
in these times. Some would even call it work.

Jeri McCormick

We can make history come alive in many ways. Any of the writing forms can do it: essays, poems, fiction, children's stories, articles, or plays. But for all of them, some research is necessary. Most of us do not have the detailed knowledge to write authentically without a look at the available sources. I recommend choosing a time in the past that grabs your attention and going to your local library to see what you can find. It will be a labor of learning like few others, a challenge in sharing historical findings augmented with imagination. It will be history with a difference, providing another lens on the enormous past that continues to drive us all.

CHILDHOOD: ANOTHER KIND OF HISTORY

I love hearing about people's childhoods. Though the stories are sometimes sad, they are often joyful and inspirational. I think of Frank McCourt's Irish memoir, *Angela's Ashes,* achingly alive and never boring. I think, too, of Russell Baker's book *Growing Up,* full of rich family dialogue, and Eudora Welty's *One Writer's Beginnings,* a quiet sensory description of how the author's early years prepared her for a life of writing.

What is it that makes this tender time in our lives so interesting? Our childhood years are our foundation, the time when we're new on the earth and being marked in so many ways. Our senses are intensely alive as we're introduced to an astounding number of things, people, places, and events. We're learning to use our bodies, learning how to get along in the world, experimenting in all sorts of ways. We're finding out that we're *people,* each of us a separate person with tasks to accomplish, choices to make, relationships to master, a language to learn.

For some of us, childhood may be the most adventurous time in our lives. Later, as adults, we may drift into patterns and routines that temper the fun and challenges we knew as children. We adults develop coping strategies, all of which are worth writing about—as any human activity is potential subject matter—but the excitement and novelty of first meeting the world may be gone, and we may find ourselves searching for ways to rekindle that freshness we knew as children. One way is to write about that time. And since childhood is always with us, somewhere in memory, we can return to it anytime.

A number of ways to approach writing about childhood are available. We're no longer children, so we're looking back, excavating our lives as we work. We might take a historical perspective, describing what it was like to grow up during the 1940s, for example: celebrating the end of World War II, playing baseball with whoever was around in the neighborhood lot; riding the streetcar with our mothers downtown; shopping at the dime store; dressing Judy Garland paper dolls on the porch swing; swapping baseball cards with playmates. Thus you choose representative activities, ones that many contemporary children took part in, recounting your own participation as an example.

In this vein, Paul Engle wrote about his family's Christmas on an Iowa farm in *A Lucky American Childhood,* 1996. It was a handmade Christmas, with a tree from the grove, and many paper ornaments made by the cousins. The gifts tended to be knit socks, wool ties, fancy crocheted yokes for nightgowns, tatted collars for blouses, doilies for tables, and once he received a polished cow horn with a cavalryman carved on it.

Jean Kerr's *Please Don't Eat the Daisies* (1957) gave us humor about her lively boys:

> The twins are four now, and for several years we have had galvanized iron fencing lashed onto the outside of their bedroom windows. This gives the front of the house a rather institutional look and contributes to unnecessary rumors about my mental health, but it does keep them off the roof. (pp. 25-26)

She went on to say that son Johnny had to have his pajamas hung on the third hook in his closet, not the second hook, and that the green beans on his plate had to be all the same length. Colin, on the other hand, had the gift of dexterity, and could take a door off its hinges in seven minutes, the towel racks from the bathroom walls in five. She expected him to become a thief, deftly cracking safes.

Another approach involves looking back with a sensitive eye on self—incidents, feelings, and relationships remembered from the early years. The concern here is not so much showing what most kids did, or what other kids in the family did, as it is to explore some key episode, speculating on how that experience might have contributed to the adult person now writing. Fred Moramarco wrote:

> Something must have been bugging my father the day I asked him for fifty cents, because although he was a sweet and gentle man and gave me most everything I asked for, this time he turns around from the sink where he is washing dishes and starts swinging at me fronthand and backhand, his face contorted with a rage I never saw before or again. I shriveled into the chair sobbing, and the silence of the rest of our lives swallows the moment forever. (From *In the Palm of Your Hand*, Steve Kowit, 1995)

A more painful example of looking back is captured in "The Portrait," by Stanley Kunitz, a well-known American poet. This poem tells about a father's suicide and the mother's inability to forgive him for that act, done publicly in a park. When the son, born after his father's death, discovers his father's portrait in the attic, the mother rips it to shreds and slaps the boy so hard that he feels his cheek still burning at age sixty-four.

Not all recorded memories of childhood are grim. A student in a class for older writers wrote about his first airplane ride, sitting in the open cockpit of a biplane. The pilot gave the only extra helmet and goggles to the boy's older brother as the three sat in the two-person plane and took off from a lake. This adventure stayed in the writer's memory for seventy years.

You can take a number of approaches when you decide to make childhood your subject:

- You can write about childhood in general, not necessarily your own, using a detached reporting style to give information or generate humor, perhaps through exaggeration, as Jean Kerr did in writing about her sons.
- You can tell about your own childhood, looking at it through young eyes, as if you were that child again. The purpose here is to recapture a bit of your past, with no attempt to bring your adult viewpoint to bear.
- You can speak as an adult looking back to garner through writing some meaning and understanding from early events in your life. This may include a child's view, but go beyond it to analysis and judgment that can only come from the adult perspective.

How, as a writer, might you get started mining your childhood as subject? Here are some suggestions:

- Give yourself a meditative atmosphere—solitude and quiet—and visualize a scene from your early years. It may be only a fleeting fragment of memory, shadowy and incomplete; even so, write about it. It's part of your conscious tethering to this world. Later, try for a complete scene and tell about the details of setting and the people taking part. Try to be a camera on the wall. Imagine what the dialogue might have been.
- Go through your belongings in search of photographs, mementos, old toys, articles of clothing, or furnishings. Use these as starters—describe them and put them in context, telling what they meant to you as a child. For example, I still have the quilt my grandmother made for my bed when I was six; I have a little girl's handkerchief illustrated with Jack and Jill; and I have some of my school photographs from fourth grade onward.
- Remember and record what you were told as a child, the rules and admonitions, the warnings you grew tired of hearing from the adults.

- Make a list of items you remember but no longer own—galoshes, perhaps, or a wagon; a locket or a sled. Keep the list for consultation when you need a subject. Include clothing, books, games, pets, whatever you can recall.
- Make a list of influences from your childhood—relatives, places you visited, playmates, sports, games, teachers, chores, radio programs, movies.
- Describe each member of your family, putting them in scenes, such as riding in the automobile or seated at the dinner table. Tell about the punishments used in your family, as well as the rewards. Tell about a time you felt humiliated or a time you felt especially appreciated and loved.

Any kind of writing is affected by the writer's roots. "Going home" to childhood helps you to know your own people and in turn to know yourself. It will lead to the "innocence of eye" you need to see things anew, as all writers must do.

Chapter 7

Focus

Jeri McCormick

We write to find out what we think. Writing freely and often, we preserve valuable memories, capture scenes of natural beauty, and put our imaginations to work. Or we might set down words with no particular aim in mind, moving with free association from one idea to another. Many experts on the writing process assert that this kind of freewriting allows us to get close to our innermost thoughts. Anne Lamott, one of our modern-day authorities on writing, advocates this kind of pen-to-paper practice as the way to achieve a fresh, spontaneous style. In any case, it leads to written pages that might never come about otherwise; all too often we wait for inspiration that never arrives.

What can you do with this output, after you've followed the advice of simply letting the words come? Now you are blessed with "raw material" to work with. It is unlikely that what you've written will be good enough in its entirety to present as a finished piece, but some parts will probably be usable, making the freewriting effort worth your while. Review the draft at hand, preferably after a lapse of a few days, so that you can return to it with a fresh perspective, and put on your editor's hat for making some objective judgments about it. You'll need to decide what form it might take. Certain guidelines can help. Ask yourself the following:

- Does the writing share an opinion, using a conversational style? Does it show the writer's mind at work, making use of the "I" voice? If personal ideas (rather than researched ones) dominate, revealing a mind reflecting informally on a subject, the *essay* form is suitable. Paragraphs will be the units that build the piece, and they will likely take the reader through a trail of speculation and subtle persuasion before drawing a conclusion.

- Is the primary purpose of the writing to share information that the writer has gained through research or specialized learning? If the primary focus is on content rather than personal musing—and the judgment of the writer stays in the background, thus downplaying opinion in order to highlight facts—then an *article* is the way to go.

- What if the written draft is peopled with characters, real or imagined, and suggests an event or situation for their personal interaction? From here, it's logical to add a suitable setting and aim for the illusion of reality that *fiction* creates. We've all lived through many stories or observed them in the lives of others; we've also imagined some, grounded in reality or not. Writing them down brings another dimension as we create a world for the story.

- Does the writing suggest an entire philosophy in a few words, packing its message with images and shades of feeling? Compression and originality of language put into a visual pattern of lines on the page leads to a *poem*. It might fit into an existing structure that has become traditional over time—such as a sonnet, haiku, limerick, or villanelle—or it may call for a tailored one-time form, known as free verse, that suits the content at hand.

DECIDING ON FORM

In working with your draft, mark the important segments that are worth developing into a finished piece. Decide which parts have energy and insight. These promising parts may be too skimpy and need expanding, or they may be too wordy and need paring down. Once you have pulled them out of the longer text and begun to focus on their possibilities, you'll be able to tailor your rewriting for what is needed. Be flexible and expect that the actual writing process will lead you in the direction that seems right. Remember that to write is to explore and to discover. Start out with a seed of an idea, gleaned from your freewriting, and stay with it. Eventually you will begin to see what form would work best for your idea.

Select one of the four forms just discussed as your goal in revising your raw material. Often you will find that you have more than one choice. For example, you may have written a reminiscence about a brother who served in World War II and came back a changed man. This could lead to an essay in your own voice about the impact of war on the individual, using the personal example; or it could prompt some research and an article on a particular battle site or army unit that shaped your brother's experience; or a story might set your imagination to working with a specific event where characters interact, one of them the brother with a changed name; or a collection of arranged lines might spin out a narrative poem, telling a bit of the brother's story leading to some poetic insight, or a distilled lyric poem downplaying the specific story but showing what war can do. Don't rule out the possibility of trying all of these options with the same basic draft. The more forms you try, the more versatile you'll become. To offer further help in choosing a direction for raw writing, here is a fuller description of each form:

Essay

One of the reasons we write is to share a personal viewpoint or to clarify it for ourselves, based on what we've seen, felt, and thought about a subject. Here the writer commits to a position and tries to convince the reader that it is valid. The noun *essay* comes from the verb *to essay,* which means "to try." The style is usually informal and conversational, showing a mind at work, meandering through an array of musings on the subject.

Reminiscences from the writer's memory are often put down in essay style, using a narrative line to tell about a particular event or person encountered at an earlier time. In this type of essay, the writer is grounded in the present, making use of current insights but examining the past in a new light. An extensive collection of these recalled times may eventually add up to a memoir, which recounts a fuller story of the author's life.

In general, the content of an essay is oriented to personal opinion and not likely to abound with researched facts, although a bit of background research may be called for to ensure authenticity of a time or place. The first-person voice carries the writing in a mode of sharing such as we might use in speaking to a friend. The writer considers ideas and shares experiences along the way, before drawing a conclusion. Persuasion, if used, is subtle, and humor often contributes to an engaging lightness of tone.

Article

When you want to present expert information on a subject, the form to use is the article. Here the first-person voice and personal musings take the background and facts dominate, employing research to back them up. An academic style of information sharing is appropriate, and footnotes may accompany the piece, depending upon the requirements of the publication for which the article is written.

For article writing, it is generally assumed that the writer will query potential publishers—usually magazines—to present credentials and suggest the proposed scope and slant of the article before actually completing it. Upon acceptance by an editor, the writer then proceeds to write and submit the article.

This form of nonfiction, fact-sharing work requires a logical order for ideas and information, and may benefit from an outline. Notes on index cards may be useful in the research stage for assembling facts, quotes, and the data for footnotes.

Personal Experience Article

Over time, the essay and the article have come to share features that result in the personal experience article. The personal opinion piece takes on an informational thrust, or vice versa, so that the result is a blend of the two approaches, with an emphasis on the writer's background as the source of information. This is often referred to as an article by the publication in which it appears.

Fiction

What if you find that you are telling about something that happens to someone? Fiction may be the way to do it. The "something" that happens becomes the plot, in which characters interact through action, thought, and dialogue, bringing some sort of change in the end. In most good stories a problem gets solved, a question gets answered, or a realization occurs. Your own life history may supply the events and/or people that make up the story. It is usually wise to change the names when real people are the subjects, and it is often necessary to supply some imagined dialogue when they interact, as well as author speculation on their thoughts, if reported. You also have the option of making up stories from whole cloth, using characters and situations that spring entirely from your imagination. In any case, you have the opportunity to introduce lives, change them, and end them. The question, "What if . . .?" is constantly useful throughout the storytelling process.

Keep in mind the basic components of a story: characterization, plot, setting, mood, and theme. All of these need attention in order to achieve a satisfying whole. When the action is over and the characters have resolved their dilemmas, reported through the eyes of one or more of them, it should be possible to recognize a theme, some truth about the human condition, and sum it up in a sentence or two. This may be a commonly held truth, written about many times over the course of history, but it should be treated in a fresh way, with a new set of particulars.

Poem

Unlike prose writing forms, where the unit of expression is the paragraph, a poem appears in stanzas and gives deliberate attention to line breaks on the page. One form of poetry, the prose poem, differs from this and casts its poetic language into paragraphs similar to those of stories and essays; but this is an exception among the many sculpted patterns, whether traditional or free verse. In defining poetry, it is usually possible to point to the line arrangement as its distinguishing attribute among the various writing forms.

Beyond the visual structure, poems make use of sound, image, and rhythm to achieve an emotional effect. All told, they seem to point beyond the words on the page to some universal truth, told in a fresh way, aiming at what is difficult to do with words. An old proverb says that "the wind in the grass cannot be taken into the house." Yet the poet tries to take the wind into the house, using sounds artfully and some well-chosen words. For the writer who wants to work with poetry, many books show the traditional patterns as well as the self-designed structures that frequently appear in modern literary magazines. Shaping form to content is nothing new, however, and is evident in the Bible and other sacred and historical texts.

After you have polished your work and attended to the details of organization, word choice, image making, and dialogue, it is time to read it aloud. This will help you to find places where you stumble or get lost in a convoluted sentence; it will reveal mistakes in grammar and usage; it will make you aware of the boring parts where focus dissipates; it will highlight the energy spots that succeed—all of which you need to know about. Unlike the first stage of freewriting when it's your own engrossed effort you are concerned with as you shut out the world and write, you are now at the point where you must think of the potential reader. What will that reader encounter upon picking up the pages you've turned out? Try to see the work through other eyes. Be the editor who knows what is good and what isn't, what belongs and what doesn't. In the appendix of this book you will find general editing guidelines.

Chapter 8

How a Poem Was Made

Karen Updike

"When you hear a sonorous line, full of hidden import, or double meanings, a line that rings in your head like a bell, you might have a villanelle by the tail." I remember a teacher telling me this long ago, and oh, how I waited for lines like that to strike a chord within me, something heart melting like Theodore Roethke's "I wake to sleep, and take my waking slow. / I learn by going where I have to go" (from "The Waking," 1953) or like Dylan Thomas's famous admonition, "Do not go gentle into that good night. / Rage, rage against the dying of the light" (1951).

Then one morning I found myself driving in an unfamiliar neighborhood looking for a high school where I had been called rather late to substitute teach for the day. I passed knot upon knot of teenagers clumped together outside gas stations or coffee shops in run-down strip malls. They were passing the time, shooting the breeze, clapping one another on the shoulder, but it wasn't time for that. School had started, and they weren't making any attempt to get a move on.

I was between jobs, unsettled and vaguely dissatisfied with my lot, so I felt a sudden rush of empathy for them, and a line, "They say they don't hurt when they can't say where," came to me like a bolt out of the blue. At that moment, I knew in my bones that, if I could just write a rhyming line that made sense to go with it to form a couplet, it would make a villanelle, a formal poem, satisfying because strong emotions are contained by the constraints of an unusually demanding pattern. The dictionary describes a villanelle as a nineteen line poem, originally in French, that uses only two rhymes and consists of five three-line stanzas and a final quatrain.

Finding a corollary line didn't prove to be that difficult. After all, they were dropouts, obviously too young to have graduated, footloose and aimless on the streets when all of their friends were engulfed in school. The line "Anyone with a place to go is already there" came readily to mind before I had reached the school parking lot.

Since villanelles have only two rhyming sounds in them, all I had to do was find one word I could rhyme six different ways and five more words I could rhyme with the end rhymes of my couplet, and I would be well on my way to making my first villanelle. The first free period my schedule offered, I set to work. It was rather like working out a crossword puzzle, fitting feelings, not just letters, into those restricting five three-line stanzas and final quatrain. I have to admit it took more than one forty-minute period, because I also had to braid the special lines throughout the poem in a regular pattern until at last they joined at the end with what would be my resounding couplet.

Of course, it would help to have something to say in each stanza, and I have to confess that what I said seemed partly dictated by the words I found to rhyme with *risk*, such as *missed, exist, resist, kiss, this.* I tinkered some more with the only other sound of the poem, using *dare, care, fair, share* to rhyme with *there* and *where,* and finally felt the satisfying click as the sounds fell into place.

Later I decided I had to use the title to set the scene, because I had not been able to do that within the rhyme scheme in the poem itself. I thought of my poem as a painting with a title, just as a seascape might be titled "Ships Leaving Falmouth Harbor." I wanted it to suggest much of the anguish and despair of adolescence without actually stating it, just as the young people in my poem could not state what was troubling them. Poems are good vehicles for saying what cannot otherwise be said.

A book that has been especially helpful to me is *Poetspeak: In Their Work, About Their Work* (1983), an anthology by Paul B. Janeczko, published by Bradbury Press. In its contributors' notes, the poets speak about the origin of their poems, and what each poet thinks poetry is and does.

Villanelle for Dropouts at 8:30 a.m.

Anyone with a place to go is already there.
At school or at home, they doubt they'll be missed.
They say they don't hurt when they can't say where.

More than most, they must know the world's not fair.
But then, who needs feelings or jobs, to exist?
Anyone with a place to go is already there.

Feeling good about themselves is as rare
As an eclipse; hiding from goals they don't dare risk,
They say they don't hurt when they can't say where.

With what flair they insist they just don't care,
Hang out on corners, dream of girls they might kiss,
But anyone with a place to go is already there.

There's nothing on earth they say they won't dare.
I know no fiction sadder than this.
They say they don't hurt when they can't say where.

The farther they drop, the harder to share;
There's little adults say they won't resist.
Anyone with a place to go is already there.
They say they don't hurt when they can't say where.

Karen Updike

Chapter 9

Using Artwork As Inspiration

Karen Updike

I had been having trouble liking my poems. Too confessional, I judged, and to what end? Too descriptive, and so what? I had done all that and then some. So had a lot of other people. Just how many ways could I describe that lonesome pine on the hill, that poignant sunset, that ruby afterglow?

For variation and inspiration, fortunately I thought back to some of the assignments I had had in poetry class more than twenty years ago. I remember being asked to write a political poem, a poem of instruction, a poem based on overheard dialogue, and then, wonder of wonderful techniques, a poem based on a work of art! Art about art! Now that was a twist. Who writes poems about art? Wasn't art supposed to imitate nature, I remember wondering, or was Aristotle wrong?

Since that time I have realized that many poets draw inspiration from painting, sculpture, music, dance, other literature, in fact, all of the arts. To judge by his poems, poet laureate Billy Collins must spend half his time in museums or the vast reading rooms of famous libraries, here and abroad. I reread his poems recently, in an attempt to corroborate how deeply I sensed his poetry was steeped in seeing paintings, real and imagined.

I especially enjoyed his "The Brooklyn Museum of Art" which begins: "I will now step over the soft velvet rope / and walk directly into this massive Hudson River painting." I myself have wanted to walk into paintings, but until I read his poem, I had not thought about writing one in which I could do precisely that. I have, however, hung landscapes where I have no windows, say over the stove, where I can now view a hillside of horses as I fry eggs, or at the foot of our bed, so we can see, first thing upon awakening in the morning, a clear woodland pool in the mountains and pretend we have been sleeping at its shore.

One further evidence of Collins' obsession with paintings in his poems, and it should be observed that his books without exception feature fine art on their covers, is that he enjoys "the world's abundance of things" so much that many of his poems could almost be seen as a kind of verbal still life. In "Study in Orange and White" he even places himself in his own "painting" of a Parisian café where he sits sipping a glass of milky green anise and thinking of himself there as "a kind of composition in blue and khaki."

But back to that inspiring assignment in which I was asked for the first time to write a poem about a piece of art. A large traveling exhibition of Norwegian art, including several paintings loaned by the King of Norway himself, was at the University of Wisconsin's Elvehjem Museum of Art, and since I was of Norwegian heritage, I thought I would check it out and perhaps find a subject for our weekly poem as well. I was surprised how intensely I was affected by the exhibit. Looking at it as possible subject material, I felt I could write about each painting, each piece of furniture, each textile. The works of art almost served as Rorschachs, calling forth emotional responses I was unaware I harbored.

Rereading now the poems I made then, one about Grandmother's bridal veil and another about a wounded Norwegian soldier being tended by his mother and sister, I see I identified with the wounded man, and perceived the elderly grandmother as bereft as I was by my sister's recent death. Describing the paintings and empathizing with them provided me with poems of mourning and a way to express a sense of futility without blatently exposing myself. It was also an opportunity to guide others to see the paintings as I saw them, a chance to be heard. In this way I was able to conceal and yet reveal what I felt, and at the time both impulses seemed equally important to me.

Since then I have also frequently used writing about art that strikes a chord within me as a means of exploring what I am feeling but with which I am not in touch. It is not unlike the way analysts explore their patients' dreams to uncover hidden impulses. When my firstborn left for college, I found myself intrigued by a bronze statue on campus showing a strong female form holding a sturdy infant who seemed to be trying to climb her body like a ladder in an effort to leave or separate from her. The resulting poem laid my frustration and conflict bare, but it was contained in four-line stanzas with tight end rhymes.

Years later when I was teaching older adult classes in creative writing, I followed in my teacher's footsteps and arranged a trip for our students to the art museum. After walking around the largest gallery for about ten minutes, we sat on wide benches near the piece of art that intrigued us. For about twenty quiet, productive minutes each described his or her choice, speculated about it, wondered "what if?" and basically tried to enter into the spirit of the works or of the artists as they created them. After a short break, during which we talked but did not formally share what we had written, we moved on to another gallery for a similar exercise. Most writers were heartened by their writing responses and went home to polish them into shape to read at our next class.

I remember writing a monologue that day directly addressing a young nineteenth-century woman in a pale afternoon dress and shawl who had a decidedly annoyed, impatient air about her. I cautioned her to look to her manners if she valued her relationship with her husband! Who, least of all me, knew where that came from? For my second poem I used the voice of the painter of a still life, as he proudly explained, in a rather overbearing fashion, his technique and how he had cleverly written his signature using a twining grapevine. Reflecting on my day's production, I was surprised to hear that a new, almost comic, tone had emerged. Gone was my customary reverence for nature, gone my anguished rehash of thwarted personal relations. I seemed to be on a whole new kick.

Now whenever I am in a rut or at a loss for something to write about, I take myself off to my ever-ready antidote and writing aid: the nearest art museum.

Charles Sprague Pearce. *The Shawl,* ca. 1900. Oil on canvas. Elvehjem Museum of Art, University of Wisconsin, Art Collections Fund and Elvehjem Museum of Art Membership Fund purchase, 1985.2.

Portrait of Mrs. Pearce

You are indeed beautiful, Mrs. Pearce
and richly deserve that plumy hat
which quite sets off your coal black hair.
And oh! The silver head
of your be-ribboned walking stick!
It must be the latest sensation.
I hate to think what beguiling things
you manage with that gorgeous shawl,
pure sacrilege, of course, to cover
shoulders snowy as yours.
Now I don't know whether you wanted to pose,
or anything else, for your husband that day,
but I do call your attention to the thistles
he chose to include in your portrait,
not pansies or roses, but thistles, Mrs. Pearce,
and quite frankly, I counsel you to look to your manners,
lest you provoke him further, for it does seem to me,
and I may be mistaken, that he has painted the darkness
of your bonnet's chinstrap more severely,
yes, indeed, rather more severely,
than any satisfied man would deem necessary.

                                        Karen Updike

Chapter 10

Writing Free Verse

Jeri McCormick

I discovered free verse as a young mother taking the afternoon off for a visit to the library. I belonged to a group of parents who exchanged baby-sitting services, and we valued that time away from the children once a week. At the library, I sat near the literary journals, most of which I had never read, and soon found myself absorbed in strange-looking texts with varying line lengths, unusual punctuation patterns and no rhyme. I thought it most pleasing, wonderfully imaginative. The following week I went back and read more.

This kind of poetry, in fluid form with no recognizable structure for rhyme and meter, is vers libre, from the French who began to favor it as a change from excessive formality. The free-verse poet has been described by W. H. Auden as "on his own," like Robinson Crusoe, doing his own cooking, laundry, and darning. The result may be strong and graceful, or simply choppy and chaotic. A good writer will manage rhythm, language, and line breaks to achieve an organic whole that seems right for the content. Such a poet is mindful of the possibilities of traditional form but chooses to use a tailored one that suits the work at hand. With no definable principle to explain the decisions made in achieving a free form, much depends upon the writer's intuition.

Free verse is not new in the history of verse writing. It appeared in the King James Bible and other writings of the seventeenth century, in William Blake's poems of the eighteenth century, and in Walt Whitman's poems of the nineteenth century, to name a few. Its popularity increased greatly in the twentieth century, with the result that it has become the most commonly practiced style among today's writers of poetry.

Within the free-verse mode of writing, some options are favored for laying out the poem's format on the page. The *end-stopped* style uses a line that comes to a natural pause through punctuation or breathtaking by the oral reader. For example, Walt Whitman used the end-stopped style in his long poem *Song of Myself* (1855):

> I celebrate myself, and sing myself,
> And what I assume you shall assume,
> For every atom belonging to me as good belongs to you.

Also common is the *run-on* style, where lines are broken arbitrarily and phrases moved on down to the next line with no concern for the conventions of prose and punctuation. William Carlos Williams achieved a long slender look on the page when he wrote in his poem "To Waken an Old Lady" (1938):

> Old age is
> a flight of small
> cheeping birds
> skimming
> bare trees
> above a snow glaze.

The poem goes on in its narrow columnlike format for eighteen lines.

While free verse allows the writer to make unfettered decisions about line breaks, it also gives the opportunity to work creatively with stanzas. Some stanzas use a same-line count for an even look (three lines to a stanza, for example). For "Rails," which appears in my book *When It Came Time* (Salmon Publishing, Ireland), I chose to use two-line stanzas (couplets) to give the look of the poem's subject, a railroad. That poem begins "The mountains stand quietly sufficient / lifting their waft of sky like broadcloth," then moves on to the next two-line stanza, leading to a total of fourteen couplets, twenty-eight lines. Other writers choose to use a varying line count to go with an idea cluster similar to the paragraph in prose. The poet Mary Oliver has used this proselike paragraph in her prose poems, some of which appear in *What Do We Know* (2002, Da Capo Press) and *West Wind* (1997, Houghton Mifflin).

In all cases, free verse is mindful of visual form, paying attention to line lengths and stanza shapes as ways to further the message and feeling at hand. It may also use rhyme in a slant way (almost rhyme), placing it within lines rather than at the ends of lines, or scattered here and there throughout the poem in no particular pattern. Similarly, it may employ other techniques—alliteration, rhythm, indentation, and imagery—to enhance the poetic language and the look of a poem.

Modern literary journals, as well as some general magazines such as *The Atlantic Monthly, Capper's,* and *The New Yorker,* many of which can be found in public libraries, will provide samples of free-verse writing. To learn more, consult references such as the *Poetry Handbook* (1982) by Babette Deutsch (listed in the appendix to this book).

Chapter 11

The Long Haul

Lenore McComas Coberly

Older writers though we are, we do write and we do get better at it all the time. Even as each of us writes in a personal and unique way, we also improve in a personal way. This chapter provides ideas for encouraging the writing gymnast who is trying to get it right, and it also holds a path with many possible detours that you will find for yourself.

WRITING IDEAS

- On my daily walks around the neighborhood, I often pass a garden that is surrounded by a high board fence. The cracks between the boards give me hints of the garden inside. As I continue walking, I keep remembering this garden, keep feeling myself walking by it. What might result?
- The curious phenomenon of seeing more as I walk swiftly by the fence than I can see by looking long through one crack might yield a metaphor for a poem. What is the difference between looking long at a narrow view and taking shorter looks at the narrow view and gaining a larger one?
- I might take note of the artful choice of color and texture in flowers, vines, grasses, and trees in the garden. If I am a gardener I might write a how-to article about using some of these choices.

- Another gardener might be inspired to write a personal essay about a remembered garden.
- A fiction writer might people the garden or imagine the people no longer there.

Fun, isn't it? Dozens of close-to-home sights are ours for the looking—a very old man planting trees; a young mother, tired and cross, bringing her two-year-old home from day care; children from the local school selling cookies or pushing Charlie's wheelchair; or Charlie's dog, specially trained by middle school children under the watchful eyes of dog training specialists—all grist for your writer's mill.

- The daily paper is life made into writing, a wonderful source for any writer. I once saw W. P. Kinsella, author of *Shoeless Joe,* eating breakfast alone in the cafeteria at the University of Iowa. He looked up as I walked by and said, "Read *USA Today* for writing ideas."
- Names in obituaries or news stories become names for fictional characters. They may even suggest a story. At the very least, you will experience a moment of astonishment at what people call their children, and that, fellow writers, wakes us up.
- The classified ads suggest situations that you can write about. They may elicit any form of writing.
- The news itself is full of plots that you can employ as you wish. Pictures from the *Columbia* space shuttle tragedy included the faces of children who had lost a parent. Perhaps you remember childhood grief or you can imagine the child's suffering to produce an essay or a children's story.
- Analysis pieces are interesting but, for writers, carry the danger of transporting us into the intellectual and away from feelings. Of course, you may be an expert who can contribute to the discussion—go for it!
- Overheard speech—on a bus, in a store, waiting at the dentist's office—may trigger memory or imagination. Go ahead, eavesdrop.
- Study a work of visual art or listen to music. You may be taken to a forgotten place, or you may want to travel in your

imagination to a never-known place. You may even want to learn about the creator of such a work and write about him or her.

- Simply select a literary form. It is an odd truth that structure sometimes frees us to express deep feelings. Read Dylan Thomas's "Do Not Go Gentle into That Good Night." It is a strict villanelle in which he pours out deep emotion.

THE REVISION PROCESS

If we write what we feel like writing, it is easier to do the necessary rewriting. An older writer once told me she had no interest in rewriting; she was "just writing for family." My response to that was and is, "What reader is more important than one's own family? Should we not do our best at all times?"

Rewriting or revision becomes a game, a challenge, if we don't get into too big a hurry. This stumbling block to writing happens when we are thinking of the finished piece or are letting other demands on us rob our writers' thought. So, okay, put the clothes in the dryer, wash the dishes, shovel the snow, and then reward yourself with a cup of coffee and some writing time to reread and rewrite. Believe me, it works.

I have given you some strategies for the long haul; you will develop others. I have taught writing to both young and old writers. The old ones are the ones who already know about the long haul. It's time to get your writing out into the world. Few things are as inspiring to a writer as a byline. Another chapter will deal with ways to get into print.

Revision involves a number of tasks that are the same for every manuscript. We must check spelling, punctuation, syntax; accuracy in names and dates is essential; the tone of the piece must give the impression we intend. Beyond all of this lies the possibility that what we have said can be said better.

I have found revision to be not a fixed task but a process. I really cannot accomplish one part until after I have finished with others. A system that works for me begins with a handwritten first draft for fiction or poetry. This is convenient when I am inspired to write while riding on a bus or waiting to see the doctor. I then copy it into type. (This can be done by typewriter, word processor, computer, or handwriting, but I need a hard copy for the next step.)

The first draft must be double- or triple-spaced to allow for writing between lines. I go over it for accuracy, inserting names and dates left blank in the first draft. Then I look for places where I have gone on too much and mark out whole sentences or even paragraphs. At this point, for me, the critical need to fill in with more writing becomes clear. I write by hand sentences and paragraphs to be inserted and mark them by number on the manuscript.

The manuscript usually needs to be recopied at this stage and is then ready for a reading for tone and the impression it gives. If it sounds stuffy or pedantic, I go back looking for where I can remove material that tells and replace it with material that shows. If it sounds cute or overly flippant, I consider finding more examples or facts to anchor it or replacing outdated and narrow language with more straightforward words. For example, *cuddly* might become *affectionate* or vice versa. When I read through, it must sound like me, the writer.

Finally, I read through the first draft and the last one checking on whether, in revising, I have lost some critical language. Some writers are afraid to revise lest they "kill" the story. This step prevents that from happening.

A clean copy ready to send to an editor or reader is a beautiful thing. As an editor I have received hand-copied manuscripts that were a joy to see and feel, but such handwriting is rare. If you need someone to copy work for you, call your local high school or technical college and engage a student to do it for you. You may even have a grandchild or neighbor who would like this small job.

Researching the markets will be covered in Chapter 15. Some tailoring to markets is necessary and must be incorporated into the revision process, but this is part of the fun. Reading market information or the publications you are aiming for is a stimulating activity. Your local library is your best friend.

Finally, you begin with a project in mind; you may even have an interested publication. You go confidently to your desk, to your kitchen table, to a picnic table in the yard, and set up your pen and tablet, typewriter, or computer and look at the blank paper before you. Your inner writer suddenly cringes and asks what you think you are doing. You have nothing to say! Writer's block has struck.

The cure, trust me, is at hand. Start writing! If you only talk to yourself, you can do it in writing. Write "I have nothing to say despite the fact that I have talked nonstop about this project for a week. There is so much I want to write, but no one is going to read anything I produce . . ." Pretty soon you will be talking about what you intend to write and the first sentence will emerge. Keep going. You can clean it up later.

If you are optimistic you will dream of great success. A pessimist will be delighted with any success, since none is expected. Either works for the writer.

Chapter 12

Ah, to See Others
As They See Themselves

Lenore McComas Coberly

As writers, we must learn to put ourselves into the heads of other people, even our repugnant characters. This probably helps everyone but, for the writer, it is required.

A recent experience of writing a nonfiction film narration about people who lived in the nineteenth century brought home to me the danger of viewing people different from ourselves as we see them, rather than as how they saw themselves. Clothing became quaint, surroundings were antique, speech repressed or overdone, and finally I failed to grasp their reasons for acting. I was reporting a view from my own time—which said nothing of interest about either time.

Histories of families sometimes contain such remarks as, "The bank was where the foundry is today." This statement does not take into account that the foundry may not exist for future readers. It is difficult to get out of our present selves, but it is not impossible.

Tess Gallagher (1986) in *A Concert of Tenses* tells us that we must "write without the bias of causes or indignation or needing too much to be right. It requires a widening of perspective, away from oversimplification" (p. 11). Stereotyping people is one of the oversimplifications we can avoid. If we catch ourselves thinking that all people in a city have a certain opinion, we are stereotyping. If we put ourselves into the head of a woman on a cold Election Day morning going to the henhouse and finding no eggs because a weasel got there first, we will likely discover that she didn't think about this special day of election at all. We can say how the population votes but not how it thinks. Even then we must remember individuals who vote in the minority and others who do not vote at all. Our woman in the cold henhouse was probably among the latter.

Closely akin to stereotyping is writing from deeply held convictions that we make all of our writing subjects share or be punished by us if they do not. Why doesn't our woman rise up and demand the vote, refuse to clean up after men all the time, write a letter to the editor demanding better control of wild animals? What's more, if she doesn't, we will make her a dull frump often seen with gingham aprons and hypertensive from eating fat in overcooked vegetables. But she wasn't us. She was herself. She leaves the henhouse, her hands aching with cold, and goes to the well for a bucket of water. In the kitchen, where the windows are covered with a film of ice, she puts water on to heat on a woodstove. But who cut the wood? Who is sick upstairs with black lung? Our frump becomes a woman of her time, not ours.

To get our characters into their time and place we have to read material written in that time and then read again and again, and we have to pay attention to detail. Our cold woman has no canned tomatoes because no short-season tomatoes had yet been developed, and she is in a cold place. Her house is red, not white, because white paint was far too expensive for a miner's family. The red paint was a mixture of lye, milk, and animal blood, a detail uncovered in your reading. How good that you recorded this note on an index card while you were reading.

Richard Wilbur (1956, p. 13), in his poem "Advice to a Prophet," tells us that we cannot imagine a place without ourselves in it. This brings up the complicated being within us—the imagination. To imagine our woman's early morning experience we must put ourselves, through imagination, into her shoes, her daily toil. We must be there with her. We must weep or be unable to weep with her. We must feel her grief, laugh at things she finds funny, feel stiff and ache in the early morning. We must feel the evening fire that comforts her. This takes time and solitude.

Don't assume that your friends, your husband or wife, or even your children won't leave you alone for the time you need to get into this woman's head. Tell them you are excited and want time alone to write. They may want to be a part of your writing; let them know that getting along without you sometimes makes them a part. Read a bit to them and see their excitement. Then face up to the fact that you are going to miss whatever it is that they are doing!

Finally, you know you have written a true story; excitement and pathos are there. But the story is twice as long as an editor will be willing to read. On to revision. No excitement there. Not so, Harry Mark Petrakus told students at a writing conference. He revises every chapter five times and at the third revision he goes back to his original and captures the words that made the story live. During the first and second revisions he corrects syntax, grammar, and the like and gets chronology straight. Then, and only then, he can go back to his original imaginative language and put it where it belongs. After that, putting it into manuscript form is rote.

This means that we must not throw away any of our writing. Keep every draft. Go back and look at language captured in early drafts. It is gold, the magic stuff of writing.

Every time we write anything we sharpen our skills, grow in our craft. The kind of writing that requires us to put ourselves into the experience of others can only make us better people. That is a bonus.

Chapter 13

The Rewards

Jeri McCormick

We who come to writing do not have to be convinced that there are rewards in store for us. We sense good things ahead and believe in writing's benefits long before actually pausing to name them. A time does come, however, when it is a good idea to consider these rewards, thus clarifying why it is that wordcrafting means so much to us.

In Chapter 1, "Why We Write," we highlighted some of these benefits. We pointed out how writing brings news of ourselves, a learning process that never ends. Writing is one of the deepest ways we have to examine our own lives; it brings answers as profound as does therapy, taking us into pain, through it, and beyond it. Writing helps show us our place in the world, who we've been and who we are now. It clarifies what we believe, gives us mental focus, enlivens our imaginations, and makes us better communicators. Learning to work with language improves our storytelling abilities, and writing down our stories widens their reach to readers beyond our immediate circles. As writers, we become creators with something to say, and we become better able to say it.

What else might we expect to gain as writers? Consider the other people in our lives and what happens when we bring to them our writer selves. We bring not only a focused mind with ideas to share but also a heightened sense of purpose. As writers, we know that we've found something important to do with our time, something that rewards us with a state of well-being and a mind-set of achievement through working and learning. We acquire new spark. Time becomes more precious because there is so much exploring to do with words. Who among your close acquaintances could not detect such a change in you? It always shows when a person is happily engaged in some activity that matters. Family members will not need to worry about their aging loved one if that person is absorbed in a writer's life. Becoming that writer, you will enjoy status and respect. You will not bore; nor will you be bored.

Another kind of belonging comes as you connect with other writers. Most communities are blessed with writers, and they reinforce one another's interest in the craft. Writers find one another through organizations, classes, readings at bookstores, libraries, colleges, senior centers, the Internet, and informal critique groups. It is good to have at least one other writer in your life to meet with regularly; if that is not possible, an exchange by mail or computer can keep you going. As mentioned earlier, round-robins mean a lot to isolated people who want to keep writing. Loneliness ceases to have a place in the life of an engaged writer.

We've been readers since childhood, never doubting the worth of our time spent with books. But coming at last to writing adds a dimension to our involvement with the ideas, plots, characters, and poems we've been encountering over a lifetime as readers. We start to read with an author's eye, asking how a particular effect was obtained. Good books become objects of study, and we seek to unlock their secrets. What are their technical accomplishments, we wonder, and what did the author do to achieve them? We look at enticing lead sentences, well-formed paragraphs, keen descriptive passages, believable dialogue, and satisfying endings; at poetic language and images, absorbing them all eagerly, assessing them, filing them away in our own "bag of tricks." Reading is satisfying as it has always been, but now it has added value.

The writer who makes time for practice on a regular basis will come to see improvement. Practitioners of all the arts and crafts—musicians, painters, dancers, photographers, and all the rest—come to that happy state of knowing they are becoming better at what they do, if they just stay devotedly focused and work hard at it. As teachers, we've seen older writing students take on assignments with determination, believing that this is the way to buckle down and learn. Most have lived long and already have something to say, but they want to say it well. And they do learn. One woman's natural wit comes through when she writes about her immigrant family adjusting to new ways and a new language; she has discovered how to select the funny anecdotes and present them with a tight, winning style. Another, who is eighty and has been experimenting with both prose and poetry, moves back and forth easily among the writing forms, turning out children's stories, free-verse poems, and personal essays. Hard work has brought her many publication credits.

Numerous older writers want to record their memories to be passed on to family members. One could undertake this project without aiming to first become accomplished at writing by simply filling pages with rambling anecdotes doggedly put together. Instead, we meet ambitious elders who want to do it well, who want to write well-crafted reminiscences that their loved ones and others will enjoy reading. Meeting these scribes of family sagas, who have taken the time to acquire writers' skills, we marvel at how fortunate their families are and what good material they'll have to read. The rewards here, as always, are for both the writer and the reader.

Declining health is often a fact of life in old age. We wish it weren't so, but it is, and we must face it as writers. Although many elders are fit and healthy, we always find a few individuals in older writing groups who are struggling with some sort of disability—impaired hearing or vision, arthritic hands and fingers, deteriorating mobility. Some carry on with all of these impairments and more. We have had many students in wheelchairs, on walkers and canes, or even bedfast in nursing homes. Yet they keep on writing. Here the rewards seem magnified, given the adversity that must be overcome. One woman nearing age ninety is bent and slow moving with her walker, but she writes. Every week she turns out stories in a shaky, uneven handwriting on legal pads—stories she can hardly read herself anymore due to deteriorating eyesight, but she finds that others are happy to read for her. She started writing in her sixties and learned how to make language vivid and concrete. She will never give it up; she cannot give it up.

What about Alzheimer's, that dread disease of the mind we all hope we'll never have to contend with? Is there anything writing can do for those so unfortunately afflicted? We can say assuredly yes, having conducted writing classes for them. I met weekly with eight such students at an adult day care center, and every week they wrote. Most could not physically put pencil to paper, but they dictated, each to a volunteer student scribe who wrote for them. I gave them a topic each week—for example, "school in the old days"—and they went purposefully to work telling their scribes what to write. They were delightful people with persistent memories, though not clear on present-day reality. We were all rewarded when I came back to class the following week with their stories typed and ready to go into their folders of accumulating work. An occasional booklet of their combined classworks was one of my projects, and handing out copies of it brought them pride to rival that of Pulitzer prize winners. If you have such a person in your life, you might become a welcome facilitator who jots down important bits of memory for that individual.

A time comes when it seems right to send some of our work to a publisher: a magazine, a newspaper, a small literary journal. For these advanced writers, chances are that someone saw and praised their work, confirming the assessment that it's time to submit to an editor. Submission takes you into the world of marketing, a pursuit you'll learn about in Chapter 15. You'll discover that persistence and patience are essential, and that rejection is simply part of the process, to be taken in stride. When you do succeed in finding an editor who likes your work, the affirmation is wonderful. Each success keeps you going, brings to you the writer's ultimate reward—something of yours in print for all the world to see.

Chapter 14

Writing Groups
in Nursing-Home Settings

Lenore McComas Coberly

I drove slowly that day. I didn't want to get to where I was
going and I knew a lot of reasons why. There was no one in
my acquaintance who had taught creative writing at the
county nursing home. I had found accounts of only two persons in my reading who had tried and neither had accomplished very much or worked at it for very long. Failure to
achieve anything was a real possibility and frightening reve-
lations of suffering and defeat seemed certain.

Those words are from an essay I wrote for a local paper which I
called "Wherein a Teacher's Ignorance Is Dispelled" and which
the editor changed to "Class Learns Value of Writing." It struck a
responsive chord in readers who very much wanted to overcome
their own fears of nursing homes.

They might not need me; but they might.
I'll let my head be just in sight;
A smile as small as mine might be
Precisely their necessity.

Emily Dickinson

Emily Dickinson might have been writing to potential writing
group coordinators in nursing homes (poem 1391). Being a part of

a group in which group members really communicate with one another is as important to the confined person as to those isolated in their own homes, but becoming a part of the larger writing community is not a reasonable goal. The writer who sees the patients as writers, takes them seriously, and shows respect for their work will soon begin to enjoy the group meetings.

The meeting room is often the sunroom at the end of the hall or a crafts room that is shared with the writers when not in use. The staff may set up tables, but it is important to arrange them so that they make a square rather than a long table. Hearing and seeing problems makes getting as close together as possible important. The square also helps the leader not seem too isolated from those farther down the table.

Sometimes when you arrive and walk down the long hall you will feel depression, like polluted air that everyone is breathing. When a problem exists in the home, it is likely to be shared by all. One such problem was created when the management of a home decided to stop cooking meals on the premises and to bring precooked food in by truck. The loss of the sounds and smells of cooking was overwhelming to the residents. It was useless to try to get them to write about that day's subject of spring and gardening. They wrote instead about their feelings of loss, and the results were taken to the officials responsible for the change. They described what it was like to line up in the hall in wheelchairs and smell food cooking, how satisfying it was to sometimes help the cooks, and how much they liked having jars of peanut butter on the table. The writing was so affecting that a compromise was reached whereby some of the food was again prepared at the home. The writer helping such a group must be prepared to change her day's plans.

At least half of the seating space should be arranged to accommodate wheelchairs, many of which can be placed close to the table so that knees fit under the table. Others may have attached tables or oxygen tanks and other medical devices. These need extra space but should be as close to the table as possible. For example, one patient with multiple sclerosis was brought to class on a portable couch.

Class members who can walk often push their colleagues down the hall in their wheelchairs. Nurses may also help to assemble the group. In spite of the most heroic efforts, some patients who can benefit from being a part of a writing group cannot come to the meeting room. The leader may visit these writers in their rooms, pick up their manuscripts, leave assignments, and return manuscripts with the comments of other class members written on them.

It is rare to find typed work in the nursing home, but seeing work in print is exciting and encouraging to the writers. The leader who types the manuscripts each week will not only come to know their work but also to understand how it was constructed. Being a writer, he or she may see in the typing the way the mind of the author has worked. It is an almost mystical experience that makes the extra work tolerable. In addition to giving importance to the student's work, the printed copy is also useful for display and for sending to relatives. It can, of course, be photocopied as needed.

Colorful folders provided at the first meeting of the group help members keep their work together and make them realize that their work is valued. Paper with wide lines and soft pencils are ideal for work done in class.

The leader needs to be friendly, sociable, and able to accept the conditions of the patients, not without sympathy but with simplicity. Beyond this, when they begin to see themselves as writers among writers, they begin to feel a part of the group.

A WAY TO INVOLVE THOSE WHO CANNOT PHYSICALLY WRITE

Perhaps as many as half of the class members will be physically unable to write their manuscripts. This has proven to be a problem but not an insurmountable one. The clear and constant emphasis upon writing, not speaking, leads even those who verbalize what they want written to focus and carefully select their material. Patients who have previously talked all the time, repeating the same story interminably, have responded well to friendly reminders that it is necessary not to say what we want to write or to have written, lest it be lost before we are ready to write.

Actual writing must be done in every session. When an assignment is made, the teacher can simply interview those members unable to write while the others are writing. Tact is required in identifying these persons since some may simply be illiterate. Take their word when they say they prefer to be interviewed. Three or four interviews can easily be conducted while the rest of the group writes, usually for about twenty minutes. If more than three or four individuals must be interviewed, you will need a helper. The interview results tend to be shorter, but they often have the quality of poetry. The interviews should be read along with the written pieces, going around the table in order, beginning each time with a different writer, whether the patient reads his or her own or has it read.

Those interviewed will include members with serious problems with sight, palsied or stroke victims, people with degenerative diseases, and those who have lost or injured their hands. In this setting the teacher needs to have developed skills in interviewing, which nonfiction writers usually have. Honest interest in what the student has to say is fundamental, but a fine line between putting words in their mouths and actively encouraging response must be always in the leader's mind. He or she must make suggestions to some people occasionally.

For example, a man who had worked as a farm laborer all of his life was unable to think of anything to say about childhood play. He had not gone to school; he had not had toys; his family had had no games or books. However, a sympathetic and creative interviewer discovered that he had known every plant and animal in the pine woods near his home. Many stories flowed from that discovery.

Another example shows the positive results of skilled interviewing: an apparently catatonic woman who had refused to raise her head responded to an interviewer's enthusiastic comments about her brightly colored dress. The patient produced a piece about her love of color and flowers. She remained an active member of the group from that time on, listening to others and smiling and showing delight when her piece was read. Others in the group came to enjoy her. One day she asked the leader to write that she liked her red dress because people talked to her when she wore it. She carefully carried the typed copy of that piece back to her room and put it into her desk.

The sounds of talk and laughter in the quiet setting of a nursing home attract visitors who are likely to remain in the hall listening. Holidays and other special events are obvious subjects for writing. The nursing-home newsletter editor is always pleased to have pieces on these subjects. Since the writing must be done well before the holiday, it is fun to celebrate in the writing class a month early. November produces Christmas stories, but others not about Christmas as well. An assignment in which each class member was given a pine bough resulted in Christmas tree stories but also in stories of winter in a logging camp. After the meeting they took their branches carefully back to their rooms. Again we are reminded of little things that matter so much when you no longer have them and how this enhanced appreciation adds to writing.

THE SUCCESSFUL NURSING-HOME VOLUNTEER

Writers who have worked successfully in nursing homes admit that it is hard work. They must concentrate and be aware of each person in the group in a way that is not required in the usual writers' group. Special problems require creative solutions. Individuals who cannot seem to attend as their fellow group members talk or read may find it possible to be still if the leader quietly walks to them and puts his or her hand on their shoulder or hand. Indeed, gentle touching comes naturally to the leader who gets along well with nursing-home residents.

Another special problem involves the individual who never stops talking. The firm reminder that it is a writing, not a talking, class, coupled with an invitation to the individual to write, takes the attention away from the talking to the alternative. Indeed, such individuals may be well focused when they write and, in time, they will find that writing helps them not to repeat themselves in speech.

If the job of leading a writing group in this setting is hard and demanding of creative solutions, it also offers extraordinary rewards. The leader can see progress where expectations are not high and comes to know the transcendent spirits of the writers as they rise above their plights through writing. It is a maturing experience to know such people and to learn from them that life is worth living for all of one's life.

The winter is past, the rain is over and gone; the flowers appear on the earth; the time of the singing of birds is come, and the voice of the turtle is heard in our land.

Song of Solomon 2:11-12

Any of the assignments given in the appendix to this book may be used in the nursing-home setting, but it is well to remember that the many objects found in a home are no longer a part of these writers' lives. A basket full of gardening objects such as seeds, tools, sand, moss, rocks, bark, and leaves spread along the tables will delight participants as well as stimulate writing. But be sure to have them write about a single object to achieve focus and keep the writing from tiring everyone. After all, some will continue writing long after you are gone.

Chapter 15

Marketing Adventures

Lenore McComas Coberly

You have been rejected! You have been told by an editor that he doesn't publish hearts, he publishes poems! No one was ever treated like this before! Right? Wrong!

First, let's revise that paragraph. *You* were not rejected; your particular, not general, piece of writing was "rejected." Even that is more harsh than the facts. An editor declined to use the piece you sent for specific and idiosyncratic reasons. *He* published something on the same subject the week before receiving yours. *She* has a problem with choosing and has a backlog three years long. They *never* publish anything remotely like what you sent. Then there is the chance that you really do need to do a rewrite, which is where *not* calling it a heart comes in.

Any or all of this may happen to you if you faithfully submit your work for publication, and every time it does you will learn something. Some editors enclose a cold and impersonal printed rejection slip. Some sign them. Some add an encouraging word, and sometimes one says, "Send me more." That is a *wow!* Do it.

If, at this point, you are saying you have no interest in publishing, just skip to the next chapter after carefully considering who you are fooling. If for no other reason, submitting makes mail time uncommonly interesting. On another level, we write to communicate. We have something to say and it requires a reader to be complete. Seeing your byline is no small reward either.

Assuming you are going to give submitting for publication a try, following are helpful mechanics to keep in mind.

1. The manuscript:
   - Use good-quality twenty-pound white paper.
   - Double-space your type and use one-inch margins.
   - Put your name, address, and phone or e-mail address on the first page.
   - Put your last name and page number on succeeding pages.
   - Always include a self-addressed stamped envelope (SASE) with every submission if you want it back.
   - Send photocopies of photographs initially, with the offer to send originals if they are needed.
   - Include a page with your name and address and a few lines about your publishing experience (optional).
   - If a publisher asks for a query, keep it to one page stating your subject and why readers would be interested as well as any expertise you might have relative to it.
   - Poetry and fiction as well as personal essays must be sent complete unless you are proposing a collection. Then send three samples.

2. Keeping track:
   - A sturdy folder for every piece of writing is a must. This can be an envelope, file folder, or, my favorite, a pocket folder.
   - On the cover of the folder write the date and the name of the publication you are sending to, followed by the date you hear from them and what they say.
   - Immediately send to another market if the manuscript is returned, noting the new date. When the cover will hold no more notations, you may want to consider revising.

3. Finding markets:
   - *Writer's Market* from the publishers of *Writer's Digest* is probably the most useful source of market listings. Most libraries have this book in their reference sections.
   - Other helpful books are *Literary Market Place*, specialized markets for children's literature, poetry, and others.
   - Lists of publications and their needs are found in most magazines for writers. I have found *ByLine Magazine, Poets & Writers, The Writer, Writer's Digest,* and *The Writers' Journal* helpful, and you may find others as well.
   - Newsletters, such as *Children's Writer,* are timely and less expensive than magazines.

MARKET OPTIONS

Newspapers: Your locals (don't forget the freebies), *Capper's, Grit, The Christian Science Monitor,* special sections of the big city papers such as Travel and Health.

Magazines: Any one that you have read and like. Do not submit to a magazine that you have not seen.

- Short stories—*ByLine Magazine, Capper's, Grit,* literary journals
- Essays—*The Christian Science Monitor, Tikkun,* your local magazines and newspapers
- Poetry—All of the above and *The Christian Century,* children's magazines, *The Saturday Evening Post* (humor), journals published by local poetry organizations

Books: Go to libraries and look for books you would like for yours to be like. That's how we found The Haworth Press with this book. Read the book section of *Writer's Market.* Talk to experienced writers or specialists in your field.

SELF-PUBLISHING

This is an honored way to publish. Walt Whitman self-published "Leaves of Grass" and many writers today are deliberately bypassing the crowded and, some say, biased publishing scene. Do not confuse this with vanity publishing, where a publisher offers to publish your book at a high price and then market it. This may mean that they will buy one ad. *You* can do that.

Remember, marketing a book is a big job. Unless you and your family and friends are willing to travel around to bookstores and keep track of your books, consider a small run. Books displayed at your local drugstore will sell if they are about your neighborhood. Histories of cemeteries, churches, schools, or historic sites will have a ready market with organizations of history buffs. Environmental groups will have a similar interest in books about the natural history of an area.

If you are aiming at one of these limited markets, it might be wise to talk with your local photocopy shop about putting the book together for you. Small printers will also do small runs of books, but they will be more expensive.

However you decide to get your writing and readers together, the rewards will be great. You will hear from people you have forgotten and those have never met. Reviews and commentary, good and bad, are exciting. Holding your published work in your hands is transcendent. Then you will lose interest and be ready to write again. I am seventy-eight and I promise you this is so.

FOR FUN AND PROFIT

The most useful course I ever took was called Article Writing for Fun and Profit. It was taught by a freelance writer who had raised a large family on the profit he made writing articles and an occasional small nonfiction book on commission. I had never published anything and was somewhat defensive about trying. (Actually, I was afraid of being rejected.)

The teacher told us up front that our best chance of being published, of seeing our own bylines, was to write and submit articles to our local papers. If something we wrote for our town paper sold, he told us, we could copy it and send it to every little paper in our state. If one-tenth of them took it for half price, well, did we know any better way to have fun?

I liked to talk with people so I began interviewing people and writing feature stories. I promised the people I interviewed that it was their story and that they would get to review it before publication (freelancers can do this). Not one ever changed a word, but this reassurance freed them to talk with me.

Finding someone to interview isn't that hard. What about the architect next door who performs with a clown ministry at the local hospital? What about the retired contractor who remembers when he first built houses with central heating? What about the farmer who keeps a few minks and sells the skins? What about the really old woman who still goes to peace marches?

Then there is the how-to article. If you helped Brownies or Boy Scouts do projects for years, remember how you did it and write for one of the craft or education magazines. This kind of writing needs to be very specific with pictures and drawings if you can provide them. I once knew a woman who tried very hard to write essays and stories only to watch her listeners get sleepy as she read them. One day she mentioned her pet spider. Pet spider! Everyone wanted to know more. Why a spider? What does it eat? Where did it come from? And what about all the Scouts who love to come and see it? She soon had not one but several bylines.

The how-to article may also be straight instructions about how to make something. Recipes are obvious, but directions for all kinds of crafts are needed. A number of woodworking magazines are always looking for project descriptions. Gardening magazines like articles that explain how to solve a gardening problem, such as growing flowers in shade or getting rid of an old stump that would be expensive to remove.

Today personal essays tend to almost overlap with articles. Personal experience, travels, family relationships, professional activities, and many other subjects are needed by magazines and papers. The more personal and introspective it is, the more likely an editor is to call it an essay. I have had what I thought was a travel article bought as an essay. The secret is to read the publication you plan to submit to and send them the kind of writing they publish.

The following article was published by a magazine for writers, but it discusses how I wrote an article for a newspaper. And I did this without leaving home!

Serendipity
Lenore McComas Coberly

Serendipity is one of those wonderful words that makes going to the dictionary such pleasure. "Something agreeable received but not sought" is serendipitous. It comes from the Persian tale of gifts called The Princess of Serendip, a name for Sri Lanka. Well, I can hardly resist going on to write about serendipity and we do seek focus, do we not?

Well, yes, focus is essential, but serendipity is magical. After my husband finally retired and began doing those extra things he had long wanted to do, he took up serious breakfast cooking (our favorite meal). One morning I walked into the kitchen to a breakfast of corn cakes and stewed apples. The corn cakes were delicious, light, thin, crisp. I commented on their quality and my husband said, "Actually, there is something different about the corn meal you got last time."

"I don't think so," I said. "It is our same brand and it is white just like before." He looked doubtful and went to the shelf for the box. Then we both burst out laughing. He had made his corn cakes out of grits! "Sit down right now," I said getting paper and pen, "and tell me how you made them. You never use a recipe and you will forget." He complied and I had this serendipitous recipe, to say nothing of a wonderfully serendipitous breakfast.

Later, in my office, I wrote an essay about serendipity and included the recipe for Grits Cakes. But this was not the end of that day's agreeable events. When I looked in my marketing file for ideas about where to send the essay/article, my eye fell on *Grit,* a weekly newspaper. Of course! Serendipity in marketing is also possible.

So my grits story found a home and I took the cook to dinner with part of the proceeds, but my thinking process had just begun. What does it take to discover, to recognize, such a happening? Being alert to happy possibilities is certainly one requirement. If I had gotten up that morning mad at my husband and determined to make him feel awful, neither of us would have seen the magic in grits cakes. I am sure I have squandered opportunities many times.

Preserving the moment is the writer's calling, but that recipe had to be gotten at once if I was to have the fun of the later writing. This kind of on-the-spot awareness may involve taking a picture, writing down a comment, or noting a recipe.

Marketing is not a favorite pastime for most of us. However, if we set a time apart for just that, it becomes pleasantly challenging. Even in marketing we must be just a little playful to discover serendipity. I was playing on the name of the publication—

Grit—but I have had other kinds of unexpected happenings in writing and marketing.

Once, when I got a short story back for the fifth time, I was preparing to mail it again when I noticed that Valentine's Day was three months ahead. Aha, the time for a Valentine story? Could I alter the story I had? Yes, I could and did by changing the party at the end of the story from just a party to a Valentine party and the title to "Will's Valentine." *ByLine* took it for their February issue. It was a better story than it had been, and I had serendipity to thank.

Finally, we must enjoy such events and we must understand that our readers will enjoy them as well. People like to hear about serendipitous events. No dinner parties are so dull that you can't liven them with stories of true serendipity, nor editors so jaded that they won't be glad to get them in writing.

You may want to try the following:

1. Remember a serendipitous event that you experienced.
2. Examine it for research possibilities. Can you tell readers how to make use of the story?
3. Go to a list of markets and read through it with your one piece in mind. See if you can find a description of publishing needs that matches what you have decided to write. If something serendipitous falls into your line of vision, jot it down.
4. If this fails, or even if it doesn't, call neighbors, relatives, or friends and ask them what experience they have had with serendipity. It will make their day and maybe give you another experience to write about.

Chapter 16

On to Fiction

Lenore McComas Coberly

As a reader I had long been aware of the deeper truth of fiction. As a writer I doubted my ability to produce such writing. As a human being with more time behind me than before me, I decided it was time to try anything I intended to try. So, in my late sixties I began writing fiction.

But beginning is specific, isn't it? I was recovering from serious surgery and spending a lot of time in a rocking chair in the sunny southwest window of my Wisconsin living room. One Tuesday morning the news was full of Black Tuesday—the stock market had plunged. It occurred to me to wonder what two of my aunts from West Virginia would say if they came to visit.

Right away I thought they would tell me they were *really* lucky because they didn't *have* any stock. A story about Black Tuesday came out of that and soon found residence in a bottom file drawer in my office. But the characters I created that day became central to a series of short stories later published in *The Handywoman Stories.* Ah, success, you say? Alas, there is truly many a slip between the cup and the lip, between inspiration and publication.

I saw the stories first as a novel and queried ten markets the first round. University of Pittsburgh Press said they published only fiction that had won in their annual contest. University of Kentucky Press said they published only dead fiction writers (the scholarly way notwithstanding, I declined to accommodate) and the University of Georgia Press expressed interest. West Virginia University Press said they had no staff! Happily, as I write this they have found more funds for their press. Smaller presses did only one or two books a year and had them already lined up. On and on. But one press had been interested, so off went the manuscript to them.

In a phone call, the then editor encouraged me with an enthusiastic endorsement. He kept the manuscript a year and then told me another book had crowded mine out, but why didn't I make it into short stories and enter their short story contest? I hastened to make the novel into short stories which, not surprisingly, got nowhere. But I had seen the possibility of short stories and spent a year ruthlessly revising them and submitting individual stories to journals. They began to be published! One was even nominated for the Pushcart Prize by the periodical *Short Fiction By Women*.

In the meantime, I got to thinking about the town I had created, which was much like the one I grew up in West Virginia. I grew curious about what an outsider would have thought of the place. There was a problem. No new people ever came to our town. After a while I thought of a possible newcomer—the state policeman sent there. So Trooper Will was born and I wrote three stories about him. Then I imagined someone rather like me going back to the town, another story. I took real events and created fictional characters to observe and tell them. All of these were short stories and many of them were published. One was even published as a prose poem.

Then I began to see it as a collection and again sent out ten queries. Two presses were interested and, to my great good fortune, Ohio University Press took it and published it as *The Handywoman Stories*. This has led to book tours, speaking engagements, readings, and contact through the mail with a wonderful group of people. One of the stories is about young "hippies" who homesteaded in Lincoln County, West Virginia. Many of them have settled there and are giving wonderful leadership to the community. They told me that I have told their story. It is interesting that I made up the "hippie" stories from my knowledge of the community after my aunt and uncle told me about befriending them.

Now my next collection is with a publisher and the tedious year of book production looms. However, that book is yesterday. I can't wait to get started on the next one. Some might say that, at my age, I had better hurry. I say writers have no age.

The Fellowship At Wysong's Clearing
Lenore McComas Coberly

"Well, Ruby Louise, it has happened. I knew it would. It was just a matter of which out-of-the-way place it would be. A bunch of hippies has moved in up at Wysong's Clearing."

"Good heavens, are you sure? There isn't any house up there."

"They went over to West Hamlin to Waggoner's Lumberyard and bought a bunch of stuff to build lean-tos to live in while they make bricks out of the clay around Adkins' pig pen!"

"I never heard of such a thing. I'd like to see how they do that."

"You're as bad as Old Man Adkins. He just let them come in over his land back around on the other side of the hill and take their jeep right up to Wysong's Clearing. They are dirty and they are strange."

"Well, they don't have a corner on dirty and strange around here, Alma Ruth, but I do wonder who sold them that land. I never thought about it belonging to anybody."

"Maybe nobody did, Ruby Louise. Maybe they're on public land and John Mayhew can make them leave. We have public school picnics up there, after all. I am going down and talk to John Mayhew at the bank and tell him we don't need filthy people living up there without the benefit of marriage. Are you coming with me?"

"I don't think so, Alma Ruth. I've been having a hard time getting rid of this cough." Which was not quite the reason but it served.

"You ought to make some steam and put Mentholatum in the water and breathe the fumes. There's no use for you to fool around what with your mama dying of T.B., Ruby Louise."

"You're right, Alma Ruth. I'll take care."

"I'll bring your mail on the way back so you can just stay in today."

"Thanks, Alma Ruth, I'm obliged to you."

After she left I got to thinking about young couples starting out new up there on that hill where you could see all across the valley to the covered bridge. It got me to thinking about my fiancé, Junior, killed so long ago at Bataan, and suddenly I was crying like I hadn't cried since the war. It seemed like I couldn't stop but I finally fell asleep in the rocking chair in the kitchen where I usually sew while I'm watching the cooking. I was nodding there when someone practically knocked the back door down.

I stumbled to my feet and yelled, "I'm not deaf. Wait a minute."

When I opened the door, I just stood there and looked. I had to take it all in. Her hair just hung. It was halfway down her back and she had a band around her forehead keeping it out of her eyes. Her skirt was made of old overall material and it hung almost to the ground. And she had on boots. Not overshoes, boots.

Don't know how long I stood there like a fool, but it was long enough to give her the advantage if she had wanted to take it. But she didn't. She just said, "Miss Ruby Louise, Aunt Addie said I ought to come and see you."

"Is Aunt Addie your aunt?"

She laughed, kind of merry sounding with her eyes squinted, and said, "No, I wish she was, but she said everyone called her that and I should, too."

"I'm a little surprised at that."

"So was I, but pleased. To tell the truth, I doubt she could see me very well." And she laughed that merry laugh again and I knew she was including herself among things to laugh at. It was then I opened the door wider and said she should come on in, what was I thinking keeping her out on the back porch.

"Thank you." She sat down at the kitchen table where I pointed.

"Now, let me get you some coffee. I was just ready myself and I have some sweet cakes."

"Oh, I want to learn how to make them for my children."

"You have children up there on top of the hill living in—" I stopped. I don't really like to be caught in gossip.

She didn't seem surprised. "Yes, I have two little girls, two and three. Hope and Charity."

At first I thought she was starting to preach or beg but then I realized she had named her little ones those old-fashioned names. "Well, those are pretty names. Uncommon, though."

"Yes, I know, but I hope they'll live up to them."

"Now, that is a fine thing, giving names to live up to. Imagine living up to Ruby Louise!"

We both laughed, and in the middle she said, "Or Jane! See Jane run!"

"Oh, oh, see Jane run. See Jane run after Spot." We laughed harder. Then I caught myself. "Is Jane your name? I'm mortified, Jane. I didn't mean to laugh at your name."

"It's all right, Miss Ruby Louise, you were laughing at yours."

"Why, that's right, Jane. Here, have some more coffee. Sweet cakes are good for children, not much sugar and you can add bran. I used to use rendered chicken fat in them but now I just get oil at the store. Don't put any cinnamon in them, that makes them taste heavy. Nutmeg is right with a little bit of lemon flavor."

"Can I watch you make them some time?" It seemed like that was a natural thing for her to ask.

"You sure can. And bring the babies. They can play here on the floor."

Suddenly I thought, *what is going on,* and it must have shown on my face because she said, "You must wonder why Aunt Addie sent me down here. Well, she said she was too old to teach me much and besides she never was that handy. But if I was going to survive up on that hill I had better find out from Ruby Louise how to do things. I really would be grateful to learn from you."

"What do you want to learn?"

"How to can and preserve berries, how to make rugs, how to get things done . . ."

"What have you learned already, Jane?"

"I went to the University of Wisconsin, Miss Ruby Louise, and I got two degrees in history. I'm a good learner," she grinned, "but maybe not very sensible, not handy like Aunt Addie says you are."

"Well, what did you learn from history?"

Well, for nearly an hour she told me about the French and all the things they tried in Indochine and how we were trying all the same things all over again with the exact same results—dead young men. I said I had never seen the sense in war, but, after all, I was a woman. She said the men in their fellowship believed like she did. Her man never registered for the draft.

"Is he a Quaker or something?" I asked.

"No, he isn't against all of anything, even war. He has to make a judgment on each one and this one he thinks is ill advised."

"But doesn't he go along with the majority—this is a democracy, isn't it?"

"He's not sure the majority want this war. Congress never declared it. Do you want this war?"

"No, I don't, Jane. And you're right, nobody in Washington asked me." We exchanged the rueful grins that it came to me women had always exchanged. "I'll help you if I can. You bring your, er, fellowship down here Sunday for dinner and we'll plan what to do."

She looked at me and said, "I'm very happy to have met you, Miss Ruby Louise."

"Goodbye, Jane," I said. "Here, take the rest of these sweet cakes to your young ones."

Jane had just started up the hill beyond my house when Alma Ruth burst in the front door without knocking. "Ruby Louise," she yelled, "are you all right?" She was wild-eyed and red in the face.

"Of course I'm all right, Alma Ruth. What is wrong with you?"

"I saw one of those hippies leaving here when I was coming out of the post office and I ran as fast as I could."

"I'm sorry you didn't get here in time to meet Jane."

"Jane who?" I burst out laughing. "And just what is so funny?" Alma Ruth demanded.

"I don't even know what her family name is—I didn't even ask."

"And what is so funny about that?"

"Well, you'll find out in due time, Alma Ruth, when you come over for Sunday dinner."

"Thank you, Ruby Louise, I would like to come and I'll bring a dried fruit cake. But why can't you tell me about this Jane now?"

"Because all the hippies will be here and you can find out for yourself."

"What do you mean, here?"

"For Sunday dinner."

She stared at me for a while. "I might have known. Aunt Addie sent them down here to you. They have been practically camping with her, taking advantage of her being so old she can't see them. Probably can't smell them either. You would think, though, that their vulgar talk would be enough even if she can't see or smell them."

"Have you ever heard them talk, Alma Ruth?"

"No, but I don't see why I should. We don't need any strange people here."

"What do we need, Alma Ruth?" I felt anger I didn't know was in me and my voice shook. She stared.

"There is something going on here. Why are you being nice to these strangers, Ruby Louise?"

Because, I thought, *what if I had spoken up against the other war, like Jane and her fellowship were doing with this war? What if Bataan hadn't happened, and Junior hadn't been killed? What if*—I was crying till I couldn't talk.

Alma Ruth stumbled over and put her arms around me. "Don't cry, Ruby Louise. I'll bring two dried fruit cakes. Those children work hard and they'll be hungry. And I'll tell them how to make chow-chow out of those green tomatoes. They put in tomato seeds instead of plants and didn't get any ripe. Don't cry, please, don't cry."

"You've been thinking about how they need help, haven't you?"

"Not till today, Ruby Louise. John Mayhew told me they were homesteading that land and it was legal and we had better get used to it if we had any sense. So I guess they've got every right to be here."

Saturday morning I stewed three chickens with onions, ready to drop dumplings in after church on Sunday. The chard and turnip tops were just cold enough in the garden to taste their best. Cabbage was crisp and I still had bell peppers to cut up with it for salad. Alma Ruth's cakes were all the sweet we needed, but I felt like it was a time to celebrate so I cooked stewed apples and opened some pickled peaches.

John Mayhew walked back from church with Alma Ruth and me, like he often does, and stayed for dinner. The young people from up the hill didn't take their jeep around the back way. They just walked straight down, stretched almost across the road there were so many of them.

Jane stood on the porch with a baby in her arms and the blondest boy I ever saw stood by her, holding another little girl by the hand. The little one was peeking out of a sheepskin hood.

"This is Olaf, Miss Ruby Louise." He held out his big hand.

"You look like a Viking," I laughed as we shook hands.

"Well, I guess I am. Kvalheim is my name. My grandparents came from Norway."

"That is sure something new for Hamlin. You all come right in. This is Alma Ruth and Mr. John Mayhew Grass."

"How do you do, Mrs. Kvalheim." John Mayhew is always exceptionally proper and exceptionally dumb on Sundays.

"I am Jane Cohen, Mr. Grass," Jane said quietly.

"Oh, of course, I—"

"Come on in, all of you," I interrupted and told everybody to take their coats into my bedroom and put them on the bed. When they got into my room they all started exclaiming at once about the quilt on the bed. Alma Ruth got so busy telling them how she thought up the pattern I could tell she forgot they weren't married.

Sally, one of the hippie women, asked if she could help me put the food on and I said of course she could. She had the nicest way of doing things, making them look just a little bit better. I don't know what that is but I know it when I see it. Alma Ruth has it too so I suspected the two of them would hit it off.

We all gathered around the big table in the dining room and John Mayhew gave thanks. Then you should have seen those young folks eat. I never saw anything like it. Baby Charity sat on my lap and chewed on a chicken leg bone. I tell you that felt nice to me.

John Mayhew asked Olaf if he had always been a carpenter. "No, I went to medical school, Mr. Grass, but I dropped out in my last year."

"Why did you do that?" John Mayhew was genuinely shocked.

"It seemed to me I had to find a simpler way to live. Making money isn't enough for me."

"Well, I can tell you," Alma Ruth was indignant, "you won't have to worry about a lot of money from people around here who haven't had a doctor since old Doc Ashworth died in 1939. We have to go clear over the hill to West Hamlin."

"Oh, I'm not licensed for West Virginia and, anyway, I'm busy building our house right now."

"Then you did finish learning to be a doctor?" John Mayhew never would let a thing rest.

"I want to hear about the house," I interrupted. "What's it going to be like?"

Thomas, the quiet small one, spoke up at last and his eyes gleamed as he held Sally's hand and talked about that house. "It will have all windows on the south and west to make it warm when the leaves drop in fall. I'm drying sassafras and walnut for the woodwork inside. The stairway will have carved posts all the way up and there'll be wooden shutters and kitchen cabinets."

"I'll make a quilt with a sassafras leaf design for your bed," Alma Ruth said. Then she blushed.

"We are honored, Miss Alma Ruth, but that will be art and we'll hang it on our wall for our children to see as they grow up." It came to me that this was a strange conversation but uncommonly interesting.

After dinner Thomas and Olaf said they and John Mayhew would do the dishes and we should play with the babies in the front room. Well, John Mayhew looked surprised but he went right along with the fun. For once, I had enough sense not to say anything.

The sun was going down by the time they left but I said it would still be light up on the hill. They said yes, they got the light first and lost it last.

When John Mayhew and Alma Ruth got their coats it felt like something needed saying. "This is a new day, Ruby Louise. It's going to be hard for those young people here but I hope they make it."

"Don't be so old-fashioned, John Mayhew," Alma Ruth had passed through all her doubts. "We need a doctor and someone who knows what to do with wood around here and if Aunt Addie and Ruby Louise approve of them, so do I."

Well, I'm slower than they think, I guess. There was a fear in me, a distrust of happiness on that hill. It didn't stop me, but it weighed me down.

"Those babies are so sweet," I said and Alma Ruth hugged me and John Mayhew cleared his throat and patted me on the shoulder as he went out the door.

I made myself a cup of sassafras tea and sat without the lights on for a long time after they left. *Carving on sassafras,* I thought, *that is going to be something to see.*

Author's notes: It was Black Monday and *The Wall Street Journal* and the radio waves were full of gloom about the drop in the stock market. Recovering from serious surgery, I was in no mood for what I was hearing. Suddenly I thought of my relatives back in Lincoln County, West Virginia—especially my aunts—and thought about how they would react, if they bothered to listen. I took up a pad of legal paper and a pencil and wrote an imaginary visit, with Alma Ruth coming to see Ruby Louise to tell her the day was a tragedy because she had heard it on the radio from Washington, DC. Ruby Louise reacts and they figure out they are the luckiest women in the world because they don't own any stock.

That particular story ended up in the bottom drawer of my desk with half-born poems, articles that turned out to be boring even to me, and ideas for "sometime writing." But I was hooked on the women and they visited me almost daily for months. The novel this excerpt is taken from, *The Handywoman and Alma Ruth,* resulted.

I grew up in Lincoln County, West Virginia, and lived there until my marriage; I listened to my grandfather discuss the coming war,

The author's daughter, Elizabeth Coberly Benforado, remembered her Great-Aunt Pearl's front porch when she read poems and stories set in her mother's hometown. It is through the magic of fiction that we are drawn into a time and place which is different from hearing about it.

knew men captured at Bataan, and heard news from the front when I went to the post office for the mail. Through the years after my marriage I returned to visit my relatives as often as I could. My parents had been killed when I was young and grandfathers, aunts, and uncles were very important to me.

So it was that I had many models for the characters, as well as the native habit of storytelling. Young dropouts did indeed move into the southern mountains, including Lincoln County, in the late 1960s and early 1970s. They often brought with them valuable education which they did not value in themselves. One of my aunts befriended such young people and stood against the more conservative members of the community who feared them. I made the young hippies in the novel Badgers from Wisconsin because, having lived in Madison since 1964 and raised four children here, I know Wisconsin young people well.

Appendix

Resources for Writers

ASSIGNMENTS TO GIVE YOURSELF

Exercise 1

One rainy morning I had just gotten my coffee, orange juice, wheat toast, and blackberry jam from the cafeteria line at the Iowa Writers' Workshop. Looking for a place to sit, I came upon W. P. Kinsella, the author of *Shoeless Joe* that became the movie *Field of Dreams,* sitting alone reading *USA Today.* I stopped in some amazement. Why was he not reading *The New York Times*? He grinned at me and said, "This paper has the stuff of fiction," and then ignored me. I sat elsewhere with plenty to think about. Ever since then I have found the everyday newspaper a rich source of inspiration for writing.

You can simply read it with your morning coffee, thereby getting into thinking words. Or you can choose something arbitrarily to write about. An article about an abused child may make you remember and write about being a volunteer in Project Head Start. A new or antique car may evoke humor about a first car, or an article on how to keep kids busy while traveling. An ad may incense you with its inane purpose so that you can create a character who is incensed in this way. If you need an exercise for a group, simply take the obituaries from a paper and let each person choose one to write from. Classified ads work also. As Kinsella said, this is the stuff of fiction. And it is the stuff of all our lives.

Exercise 2

Make a "linked image" poem in which you show how you feel and what you are thinking mainly by the images you select to include. Take out any lines of explanation or philosophy if they have crept in. Let the collage of images, and their order, give the impression and make the point. Images collected on a spring walk, or a night in your garden, or from a carnival, a farm auction, or a family picnic have all been used to good effect as linked image poems. Most writers say that they are never without a notebook for jotting down images and ideas. Mary Oliver has admitted to hiding pencils in trees along the path of some of her favorite walks! Some writers prefer index cards which they keep in a shirt pocket or purse.

Exercise 3

Do you remember a day when your parents took the time to play some sort of imaginative game, or sing, or tell you stories, or read to you? Go into detail about what the experience was and why it was so memorable for you.

Exercise 4

Stories from childhood offer a common heritage we can draw on for subject matter. Interpreting those stories in a new way to draw modern-day lessons from them, or embellishing them for the sake of humor can lead to an engaging piece of writing.

Choose a story or nursery rhyme from the following list (or one from your memory) and write what comes to mind. Feel free to move the characters around, plucking them from one story to go in another, or continue with a given story, imagining what happened next (Goldilocks as an adult, for example). Try using the "I" voice and *be* the character you choose. Or try using the *rhythm* of a nursery rhyme to accompany your own words. The possibilities are many; use them to give yourself multiple assignments.

Goldilocks and the Three Bears	Jack Be Nimble
The Three Little Pigs	Little Miss Muffet
The Little Red Hen	Jack and Jill
Snow White and the Seven Dwarfs	Little Boy Blue
Pinocchio	Baa Baa Black Sheep
Cinderella	Simple Simon
Rapunzel	Little Tommy Tucker
Hansel and Gretel	Mary Had a Little Lamb
Billy Goats Gruff	Little Bo Peep

Rumpelstiltskin
Little Red Riding Hood
Sleeping Beauty

Jack Sprat
Peter, Peter Pumpkin Eater
Old Mother Hubbard

For an example of work with fairy tales, see Ann Sexton's *Transformations* (Houghton Mifflin Co.).

Exercise 5

Think about the color black, then the color white, and, finally, black and white. Write about one of them, reporting whatever comes to mind. Look at what you have written. Is it a poem being born? Poetic prose that may become an essay? An inspirational article? Or information about using these colors in artwork? Keep writing. See where it goes. No subject is forbidden except one that does not come from you, the writer.

Exercise 6

Think of two or three things—they could be objects or events or processes—that you find really exciting. Choose one and describe it in the present tense. Make it more and more exciting as you go along. Repeat words. Put in verbal exclamations. Invert word order to show your increasing excitement. Events such as seeing trees budding, being pushed in a swing, hearing a wren sing, watching a glassblower, having cousins come to visit, receiving a prize, or hearing a performance of music are just a few possible ideas. This assignment usually results in a poem, the language of strong feeling.

Exercise 7

Our sense of smell may be the most primitive. It is believed that the first sense developed in the fetus is this one, and that is why it evokes such deep emotional response from us. Arthur Hasler, who discovered that fish find their way back to their spawning grounds using their sense of smell, wrote that he got this idea when he walked onto a lake's edge when wildflowers were in bloom and found himself transported to the lakeside of his childhood. He did not just remember this place, but memory came back whole. He was there.

Working alone or with others, get a box of cinnamon, a jar of Vicks VapoRub, some paste shoe polish, a fragrant rose, a peony, some pine pitch, some fresh cut grass or newly dug earth, and, without talking, begin to write about what you think when you have smelled one of these materials. Then write from a second olfactory experience, if the first proved tepid. We have rarely seen a writer who did not discover important and valid writing material in this way.

What you write may be a poem, an essay (the most likely in our experience), or the beginning of fiction.

Exercise 8

Survey through the teachers you have had in your lifetime who taught you how to make something well or how to think about something in a new and constructive way. The subject could range from making good piecrust to thinking about politics or religion differently. Choose one teacher from whatever level you please and describe the teacher, the setting, and the learning session as completely as possible. Try to suggest how this contact and experience affected how you have come to live your life.

Exercise 9

A camera catches something of life and holds it for later viewing. The resulting photograph is a reminder of that moment captured; it is an instant fixed, set down and held. Often we can see in a photo something we did not observe in life at the time, though we were present at the scene. Similarly, a photo gives us the chance to see something that was not part of our own lived experience. Writing from a photograph can take you back to a place where you've been, or it can show you something you've never seen before. Try the following:

- Consult your family photograph collection, selecting five portraits, individual or group shots. Use each as a starting point, writing whatever comes to mind. Give each picture about five minutes. Put away your five drafts and return to them later, the next day, perhaps, selecting the two drafts that seem most promising as writing subjects. Give the two drafts a careful review and rewrite each, going deeper this time to create a story, poem, or essay. Feel free to speculate, filling in with imagined details if you don't know the actual details.
- Look through magazines (*Doubletake* is a good one, or *National Geographic*) or books of photographs at the library, selecting a picture that catches your eye. People, places, animals, interiors—all are potential subjects for writing. As in the previous exercise, choose five to work with at the outset and narrow down the possibilities to two for further treatment. Again, go beyond surface description and try to create a small world for each of the two pictures.

Exercise 10

Describe something that has been abandoned, such as a house, an old schoolhouse, a farmyard, a rural church, a sandlot ball diamond, the site of a summer day camp, a main street, the town square, a place which you knew well when it was vibrant and thriving. Use your mind as a movie camera, panning from place to place, and remembering.

Exercise 11

Space is never empty, even if we fill it with memory or dreams. Imagine walking down a hallway and entering a door; then write what you see and what happens there. I once asked a retired surgeon to do this and he wrote about opening the door and confronting a family he had to tell that their loved one had died on the operating table. He had never told anyone about this before. His wife told me she understood him in a way she had not before when she read this piece of writing.

A variation of this exercise is to look out a window and write about one thing you see. Another is to look around the room you are in and write about any one thing in it.

Then, after any of these exercises, write about something that is *not* in the room, out the window, along the hall. One writer looking out an urban window wrote about the newsstand below. Then, when asked to write about what was not there, he wrote about his time as a newsboy, before coin-operated machines. Later, another member of the writing group wrote about her brother who sold a newspaper to Mark Twain on a St. Louis street. She had been inspired by a fellow writer. It happens.

Exercise 12

Create and describe a place that is like the way you feel sometimes—happy or gloomy, fearful or joyous, full of revenge or loving acceptance. Describe it, name it, give the directions about how to get there, and tell how long you have been there. Invite someone to join you there, or warn him or her away from the place. It is your choice.

Exercise 13

One starting point to elicit a writing draft is to closely observe a defined area within the writer's field of vision. Standing at a window, for example, you would look for details outside, moving the eye to all points visible within the window frame. After a careful look of perhaps two minutes, you sit down and write what comes to mind, based on one or more of the objects observed.

A variation on this assignment is to study the defined area as described, but to write about something *not* present during the observation. It might be something that it would be reasonable to expect in that particular scene—a bird feeder, for example, in a neighborhood where most yards have them; or it might be something imagined for the sake of speculation or whimsy—a flock of flamingos, say, or a Ferris wheel in a residential yard.

Observe one of the following for two minutes, then sit down and write something *not seen*. Write for five minutes. Put the draft away for a day or two before reviewing it for possible further work. Return to the list when you need a new writing subject.

- *A window:* Try different windows facing different scenes. Your front window may face a street, for example, while a back bedroom window may face a convergence of backyards.
- *A mirror:* What does the mirror capture in addition to your own image?
- *A cabinet drawer:* Choose one that contains a variety of objects. A dresser drawer, or any other drawer, will work for this.
- *A closet:* Stand at the door and look in.
- *A garage:* Stand at the door and look in.

Exercise 14

Think about a time when your parents, or teacher, or coach disappointed you in some way. What did it feel like? How did others feel about it? What did you do about it? Did the person know of your disappointment? Or you might think of a time when you disappointed one of these people. These situations often make good material for stories.

Exercise 15

Food is such an important part of human experience that we cannot do any kind of writing without including it. Reviewers of restaurants, magazine food writers, and cooks who write about recipes for special nutritional needs have an obvious connection to food. You may be such a person, but other less specialized writers need to be fluent about food as well.

Imagine a meal. Describe the menu, what it looks like, how it smells, how it tastes, and even what it sounds like. At an elegant banquet in

Shanghai one of my Chinese hosts told me, with a smile, that food should be beautiful to see, fragrant to smell, and delicious to hear. Then he demonstrated a deep sigh of pleasure.

Remember or imagine people eating food you have described. What do they say? Do they appreciate the cook? Are they happy, worried, or silent? You have started a short story! Keep going.

Your life experience may have endowed you with special knowledge or skill with food. Write about the meal from the point of view of a busy housewife or househusband preparing it. That could be helpful to others if it became an article, or it could become humorous, ending with a trip to the deli! You might also write about just one food in this way. Is your mouth watering? So is mine.

Exercise 16

Talk directly to a beloved child who is sleeping, and tell him all the things you hope he will learn, experience, solve and enjoy in life. Of course we all know a child would neither comprehend or sit still for a long, serious, one-way conversation, but this piece of writing will reflect you, your life and values, which you hope to communicate and pass on to him in other ways as he grows up and comes to know you. It could also be among the tangible things you leave for him when you pass on. Poems or essays may result, light-hearted or serious, always wise.

Exercise 17

Water is always with us. It is one of the elements that keeps us alive on the planet. For this assignment, stop to think about the ways we experience water in our lives. We drink it, of course, and our bodies are largely made of it. What else? Think about water in the environment—rivers, streams, ponds, lakes, oceans. What about the garden hose and the kitchen sink? Dew on the grass and frost on the bushes?

A technique that often helps in organizing thoughts for a writing session involves the use of "clustering." It employs word association to build a pattern of related ideas that is freer and less structured than the traditional hierarchical outline. Taking off from a central theme, the cluster builds outward in all directions to create a pre-writing map. A detailed description of this technique appears in *Writing the Natural Way* (1983) by Gabriele L. Rico. Try it, using "water" as the central focus. Give yourself five minutes to branch out with your associations, and then write a draft using the completed cluster. Choose the most appealing items, not necessarily all of them. Here is a sample, showing one writer's cluster built around "water."

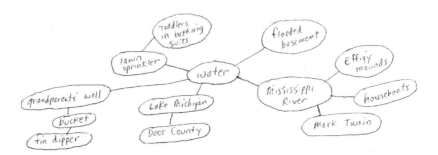

Exercise 18

Choose something you know a great deal about, something you make well or take care of well. Write fully about this activity. *But* be sure to tell an obvious lie in almost every sentence! Minimize, exaggerate, stretch the truth however you can. The resulting articles or poems will be amusing as well as informative. Some subjects writers have used were how to prepare a plot for a vegetable garden, how to run a small community movie theater, how to coach a sport for young people, and how to take care of a dairy herd.

Exercise 19

A collection of objects scattered on a table will start a lot of conversations for a group, but to evoke writing each person must choose a single object and begin writing about what it makes him or her think, remember, or hope. If you are writing alone and want a fresh start, simply look around the room in which you are writing, choose an object, and begin writing. A postal scale may lead to a story about a war bride trying to cook from American recipes that do not give ingredients by weight. A dull pencil may make you feel like the shy child you were in third grade. Or an object you suddenly remember that is not there may move you to poignant memory. Then write until you get somewhere.

It is important to recognize, in any writing, that your beginning may be just for getting started and needs to be discarded once you get into what you want to write. Be sure not to fall in love with every word you write! In the different light of another day you will be able to revise, add, subtract, and polish, but don't throw away that first draft! You are sure to need to go back to it before you finish revising.

Exercise 20

Write instructions telling how to do something for which, to your knowledge, there have never been any instructions written in the world. Such topics might include how to be happy, how to choose an imaginary pet, how to be overlooked when teams are chosen, how to find the cake recipe your father says his auntie always made for him.

Exercise 21

The story of your life is a resource you'll turn to time and again. Here is one way to go about using it. Fold a sheet of paper in half lengthwise, and then lengthwise again, to form four vertical columns (or draw vertical lines on the sheet). Label the columns as follows: Places, People, Objects, Events. Within the categories, list what comes to mind as you think back over your life. Where did you go? Who were some of the key people in your life? What objects mattered to you? What events do you remember? Don't worry about making these lists comprehensive; you can always use this assignment again another day to generate more material for writing. Give yourself about three minutes for each list, and you'll be ready to review the page in about twelve minutes.

Now begin writing your draft, choosing randomly from all four columns. You don't need to write about every item you've listed. Start with the phrase, "I'm from . . ." and include your choices, interspersing "I'm from . . ." periodically as you go. Bring in the senses and any related details as you write. Don't worry about grammar, punctuation, or layout on the page. Just write.

Here is a sample, to illustrate the list making:

Places	People	Objects	Events
School playground	Piano teacher	Winter galoshes	Sixth-grade play
Rollman's Dept. Store	Cousin Nell	Blue bicycle	High school graduation
Fruit cellar	Sweetie Jackson	Box of paints	Birth of brother

This writer, working from the list, might begin, "I'm from the top of the monkey bars on the asphalt playground, from ugly zip-up galoshes and baggy snowpants; I'm from a bad case of stage fright in the sixth-grade play, from the bargain basement in Rollman's . . ."

EDITING CHECKLIST

In assessing a draft, ask yourself several questions as you go through the rewrite stage. Here are some basic ones:

- Is the lead paragraph enticing? Does it move quickly into the essential message or story? In the case of poetry, does the first line pull the reader in? Beginning with an anecdote or dialogue may enhance your prose.
- Is the writing free of unnecessary words or phrases? Watch out for overwriting. In the case of poetry, especially, use no word that does not contribute to the message.
- Does the language contain any overused words or phrases, inappropriate slang, or clichés? Such writing seems tired, lazy, or perhaps too cute.
- Does the writing *show* emotion rather than simply tell about it? Don't say you are sad; produce a tear.
- Are there any intrusions by the author that shouldn't be there? You will need to learn when your own observations belong, as perhaps in an essay, or do not belong, as in a story where the characters themselves are on stage, not the author.
- Are the verbs active and precise? Look at each verb and ask if that is precisely the right one to do the work you need done. Nouns and verbs are especially important in any piece of writing. Use them for employing the senses.
- Are the adjectives and adverbs well chosen and sparingly used? Too many modifiers weaken one another and the verbs and nouns they modify. In poetry, use metaphors and similes to make comparisons.
- Is there variety in sentence length? Avoid using all long sentences or all short sentences; you need some of each. Poetry, on the other hand, may call for unity in line length for the sake of a desired structure or for rhythm.
- Is the organization satisfactory, with the elements of the piece coming in the right order? You may need to experiment with rearranging sentences, paragraphs, or poem lines and stanzas to achieve the best effect.

- Does the ending occur at the right place and provide a satisfactory closure to what has come before?

MARKETING INFORMATION

You will find help in locating markets for your work in writer's magazines, in marketing books such as *Writer's Market* and *Literary Market Place,* and in your own reading. Read widely as if doing a marketing survey at your library and you will find markets we have never heard of or do not mention here. The following list, though not exhaustive, includes markets we have found friendly:

1. *Bibliophilos,* Dr. Gerald J. Bobango, editor, The Bibliophile Publishing Co., Inc., 200 Security Bldg., Fairmont, WV 26554
2. *ByLine Magazine,* Marcia Preston, editor and publisher, P.O. Box 5240, Edmund, OK 73083-5240
3. *Capper's,* Ann T. Crahan, editor (the same address as *Grit*)
4. *The Children's Writer,* 95 Long Ridge Rd., West Redding, CT 06896-0811
5. *The Christian Century,* 104 S. Michigan Ave., Suite 700, Chicago, IL 60603
6. *The Christian Science Monitor,* Home Forum Page, One Norway St., Boston, MA 02115
7. *Grit,* Donna Doyle, editor in chief, 1503 SW 42nd St., Topeka, KS 66609-1265
8. *Nimrod,* Francine Ringold, editor, The University of Tulsa, 600 S. College, Tulsa, OK 74104-3189
9. *Poets & Writers Magazine,* 72 Spring St., New York, NY 10012
10. Publications of local and state writers' organizations
11. Local newspapers
12. Local publications for older readers
13. Regional newspapers published in the region you remember from childhood, for example, *Blue Ridge, Arizona Roads,* and any local newspaper
14. Anthologies that put ads in the back of *Poets & Writers Magazine* (We found one that wanted previously published poems and another about experiences in China!)

Recommended Reading

BOOKS

Addonizio, Kim and Dorianne Laux. *The Poet's Companion: A Guide to the Pleasures of Writing Poetry.* New York: W.W. Norton and Company, 1997.

Albert, Susan Wittig. *Writing from Life: Telling Your Soul's Story.* New York: Jeremy P. Tarcher/Putnam, 1996.

Aronie, Nancy Slonim. *Writing from the Heart: Tapping the Power of Your Inner Voice.* New York: Hyperion, 1998.

Bender, Sheila. *Writing Personal Essays: How to Shape Your Life Experiences for the Page.* Cincinnati, OH: Writer's Digest Books, 1995.

Bernays, Anne and Pamela Painter. *What If? Writing Exercises for Fiction Writers.* New York: HarperCollins, 1990.

Bradbury, Ray. *Zen in the Art of Writing.* Santa Barbara, CA: Capra Press, 1990.

Brande, Dorothea. *Becoming a Writer.* New York: Jeremy P. Tarcher/Putnam, 1981.

Brooks, Cleanth and Robert Penn Warren. *Understanding Poetry.* Fort Worth, TX: Harcourt College Publishers, 1976.

Browne, Renni and Dave King. *Self-Editing for Fiction Writers.* New York: HarperPerennial, 1994.

Deutsch, Babette. *Poetry Handbook.* New York: Grosset and Dunlap, 1982.

Dillard, Annie. *The Writing Life.* New York: Harper and Row, 1990.

Elbow, Peter. *Writing Without Teachers,* Second Edition. New York: Oxford University Press, 1998.

Engle, Paul. *A Lucky American Childhood.* Iowa City: University of Iowa Press, 1996.

Esbensen, Barbara. *A Celebration of Bees: Helping Children Write Poetry.* Winston Press, 1975.

Fox, John. *Finding What You Didn't Lose: Expressing Your Truth and Creativity Through Poem-Making.* New York: Jeremy P. Tarcher/Putnam, 1995.

Gallagher, Tess. *A Concert of Tenses.* Ann Arbor, MI: University of Michigan Press, 1986.

Gardner, John. *The Art of Fiction: Notes on Craft for Young Writers*. New York: Vintage Books, 1991.

Goldberg, Bonni. *Room to Write: Daily Invitations to a Writer's Life*. New York: Jeremy P. Tarcher/Putnam, 1996.

Goldberg, Natalie. *The Long Quiet Highway*. New York: Bantam, 1994.

Goldberg, Natalie. *Wild Mind: Living the Writer's Life*. New York: Bantam Books, 1990.

Goldberg, Natalie. *Writing Down the Bones: Freeing the Writer Within*. Boston, MA: Shambhala Publications, 1986.

Hall, Donald. *Claims for Poetry*. Ann Arbor, MI: University of Michigan Press, 1982.

Hall, Donald. *Writing Well*. New York: Little Brown and Company, 1979.

Heffron, Jack. *The Writer's Idea Book*. Cincinnati, OH: Writer's Digest Books, 2002.

Hollander, John. *Rhyme's Reason*. Stamford, CT: Yale University Press, 2001.

Jackson, Jacqueline. *Turn Not Pale, Beloved Snail: A Book About Writing Among Other Things*. New York: Little Brown and Company, 1974.

Janeczko, Paul B. *Poetspeak: In Their Work, About Their Work*. New York: Bradbury Press, 1983.

Kelton, Nancy Davidoff. *Writing from Personal Experience: How to Turn Your Life into Salable Prose*. Cincinnati, OH: Writer's Digest Books, 2000.

Kerr, Jean. *Please Don't Eat the Daisies*. Garden City, NY: Doubleday, 1957.

King, Stephen. *On Writing: A Memoir of the Craft*. New York: Scribner, 2000.

Kowit, Steve. *In the Palm of Your Hand: The Poet's Portable Workshop*. Gardiner, ME: Tilbury House, Publishers, 1995.

Kumin, Maxine. *To Make a Prairie*. Ann Arbor, MI: University of Michigan Press, 1979.

Kunitz, Stanley. *The Poems of Stanley Kunitz, 1928-1978*. New York: W. W. Norton and Co., 1971.

Lamott, Anne. *Bird by Bird: Some Instructions on Writing and Life*. New York: Pantheon, 1995.

Le Guin, Ursula K. *Steering the Craft: Exercises and Discussions on Story Writing for the Lone Navigator or the Mutinous Crew*. Portland, OR: The Eighth Mountain Press, 1998.

Lerner, Betsy. *The Forest for the Trees: An Editor's Advice to Writers*. New York: Riverhead Books, 2000.

Lodge, David. *The Art of Fiction*. New York: Viking Press, 1994.

Maisel, Eric. *Deep Writing: 7 Principles That Bring Ideas to Life.* New York: Jeremy P. Tarcher/Putnam, 1999.

Minot, Stephen. *Three Genres: The Writing of Poetry, Fiction, and Drama.* New York: Prentice-Hall, 2002.

O'Conner, Patricia T. *Words Fail Me.* New York: Harcourt, 1999.

Oliver, Mary. *A Poetry Handbook.* New York: Harcourt, 1995.

Oliver, Mary. *West Wind.* Boston: Houghton Mifflin, 1997.

Oliver, Mary. *What Do We Know.* Cambridge, MA: Da Capo Press, 2002.

Olsen, Tillie. *Silences.* New York: Feminist Press, City University of New York, 2003.

Paterson, Katherine. *The Gates of Excellence.* New York: Elsevier/Nelson, 1981.

Peck, Robert Newton. *Secrets of Successful Fiction.* Cincinnati, OH: Writer's Digest Books, 1980.

Peterson, Franklynn and Judi Kesselman-Turkel. *The Magazine Writer's Handbook.* New York: Dodd, Mead and Company, 1982.

Plotz, Helen. *Eye's Delight: Poems of Art and Architecture.* New York: Greenwillow Books, 1983.

Powell, Dannye Romine. *Parting the Curtains; Interviews with Southern Writers.* Winston-Salem, NC: John F. Blair, Publisher, 1994.

Provost, Gary. *Make Your Words Work: Proven Techniques for Effective Writing—For Fiction and Nonfiction.* Cincinnati, OH: Writer's Digest Books, 2001.

Rainer, Tristine. *Your Life As Story.* New York: Jeremy P. Tarcher/Putnam, 1997.

Reeves, Judy. *Writing Alone, Writing Together.* Novato, CA: New World Library, 2002.

Rico, Gabriele. *Writing the Natural Way.* New York: Penguin Press, 2000.

Safire, William and Leonard Safire, eds. *Good Advice on Writing.* New York: Simon and Schuster, 1992.

Sexton, Ann. *Transformations.* New York: Houghton Mifflin, 2001.

Stafford, William. *Writing the Australian Crawl.* Ann Arbor, MI: University of Michigan Press, 1978.

Stafford, William. *You Must Revise Your Life.* Ann Arbor, MI: University of Michigan Press, 1986.

Strunk, William Jr. and E.B. White. *The Elements of Style,* Fourth Edition. Needham Heights, MA: Allyn and Bacon, 2000.

Ueland, Brenda. *If You Want to Write: A Book About Art, Independence and Spirit,* Tenth Edition. Saint Paul, MN: Graywolf Press, 1997.

Welty, Eudora. *One Writer's Beginnings.* Cambridge, MA: Harvard University Press, 1984.

Whitman, Walt. *Complete Poetry and Selected Prose.* Cambridge, MA: Houghton Mifflin, 1959.

Wilbur, Richard. *Advice to a Prophet.* New York: Harcourt Brace, 1961.

Williams, W. C. *Selected Poems.* New York: New Directions, 1968.

Wooldridge, Susan G. *Poemcrazy: Freeing Your Life with Words.* New York: Clarkson Potter, 1996.

Ziegler, Alan. *The Writing Workshop,* Volumes I and II. New York: Teachers & Writers Collaborative, 2000.

PERIODICALS

ByLine Magazine. Marcia Preston, editor: P.O. Box 5240, Edmund, OK 73083-5240.

The Writer. Elfrieda M. Abbe, editor: Kalmbach Publishing Company, 21027 Crossroads Circle, P.O. Box 1612, Waukesha, WI 53187-1612.

Writer's Digest. Kelly Nickell, editor: 4700 E. Galbraith Rd., Cincinnati, OH 45236.

The Writers' Journal. Leon Ogroske, editor: Val-Tech Media, P.O. Box 394, Perham, MN 56573-0394.

REFERENCE BOOKS

The International Directory of Little Magazines and Small Presses. Paradise, CA: Dustbooks.

Literary Market Place. Medford, NJ: Information Today, Inc.

The Writer's Market. Palm Coast, FL: Writer's Digest Books.

Index

Order a copy of this book with this form or online at:
http://www.haworthpress.com/store/product.asp?sku=5192

WRITERS HAVE NO AGE
Creative Writing for Older Adults, Second Edition

_____in hardbound at $29.95 (ISBN: 0-7890-2468-3)

_____in softbound at $19.95 (ISBN: 0-7890-2469-1)

Or order online and use special offer code HEC25 in the shopping cart.

COST OF BOOKS_____

POSTAGE & HANDLING_____
(US: $4.00 for first book & $1.50
for each additional book)
(Outside US: $5.00 for first book
& $2.00 for each additional book)

SUBTOTAL_____

IN CANADA: ADD 7% GST_____

STATE TAX_____
(NJ, NY, OH, MN, CA, IL, IN, & SD residents,
add appropriate local sales tax)

FINAL TOTAL_____
(If paying in Canadian funds,
convert using the current
exchange rate, UNESCO
coupons welcome)

☐ **BILL ME LATER:** (Bill-me option is good on
US/Canada/Mexico orders only; not good to
jobbers, wholesalers, or subscription agencies.)
☐ Check here if billing address is different from
shipping address and attach purchase order and
billing address information.

Signature_____

☐ **PAYMENT ENCLOSED: $**_____

☐ **PLEASE CHARGE TO MY CREDIT CARD.**

☐ Visa ☐ MasterCard ☐ AmEx ☐ Discover
☐ Diner's Club ☐ Eurocard ☐ JCB

Account # _____

Exp. Date_____

Signature_____

Prices in US dollars and subject to change without notice.

NAME_____

INSTITUTION_____

ADDRESS_____

CITY_____

STATE/ZIP_____

COUNTRY_____ COUNTY (NY residents only)_____

TEL_____ FAX_____

E-MAIL_____

May we use your e-mail address for confirmations and other types of information? ☐ Yes ☐ No
We appreciate receiving your e-mail address and fax number. Haworth would like to e-mail or fax special
discount offers to you, as a preferred customer. **We will never share, rent, or exchange your e-mail address
or fax number.** We regard such actions as an invasion of your privacy.

Order From Your Local Bookstore or Directly From
The Haworth Press, Inc.
10 Alice Street, Binghamton, New York 13904-1580 • USA
TELEPHONE: 1-800-HAWORTH (1-800-429-6784) / Outside US/Canada: (607) 722-5857
FAX: 1-800-895-0582 / Outside US/Canada: (607) 771-0012
E-mailto: orders@haworthpress.com

For orders outside US and Canada, you may wish to order through your local
sales representative, distributor, or bookseller.
For information, see http://haworthpress.com/distributors

(Discounts are available for individual orders in US and Canada only, not booksellers/distributors.)

PLEASE PHOTOCOPY THIS FORM FOR YOUR PERSONAL USE.
http://www.HaworthPress.com   BOF04